MW01255149

GHOST MOUNTAIN

GHOST MOUNTAIN

Rónán Hession

Bluemoose

First published in 2024 by
Bluemoose Books Ltd
25 Sackville Street
Hebden Bridge
West Yorkshire
HX7 7DJ

www.bluemoosebooks.com

British Library Cataloguing-in-Publication data
A catalogue record for this book is available from the British Library

Hardback 978-1-91569-313-6

Printed and bound in the UK by Gomer

This book is dedicated to my wife, Sinéad,
with all my love, always.

BOOK 1

Ghost Mountain

It was, in the ordinary sense of the word, a mountain. Emerging from the surrounding unfamous landscape, it was higher than all around it, though not very high. Limpet-shaped, its crest was bare and rounded, like a knee. It faced in all directions without preference, as mountains do. It obstructed both light and wind, but so too did it bring out their personalities. Light, accommodating and peaceful, addressed the mountain with shade and contrast, whereas wind, which is never the same twice, often became exercised by it. From one aspect there appeared to be two hollows, sitting like sunken sockets about halfway up its slope. A third hollow lay between but below the first two, creating what looked like a haunted expression, though the mountain did not, strictly speaking, ever express itself. When the time came to give it a name, it would be called Ghost Mountain because of those hollows.

To say that the mountain was this or that. To ascribe it physical or metaphysical characteristics. To describe it in a way that separated it from everything that was not it – these are all habits of the human mind, and so, it could justifiably be said that all and any such remarks described the describer more than Ghost Mountain. Ghost Mountain had no mind. It did not describe itself. It had no self or self-view. Ghost Mountain was Ghost Mountain.

All we know is that it appeared yesterday.

Ocho

Ocho was looking at his wife. At that moment, it was unfathomable to him how truly separate another person was.

Her name was Ruth.

She was reading her phone and held it with both hands as though she were reading a book.

The soup she had made was on the table in front of them. Ocho had started his soup without waiting for her.

As he was looking at her, he thought about how she wasn't thinking about him. About how this thought connected him to her and separated her from him. This mattered to him in a new and important way. Where exactly did it matter to him, bodily speaking? He checked inside himself. There was something in his gut, among the organs that were jammed in there. His thoughts and his gut seemed connected. The gut was a second brain, it was said, and had more neurons than a rat's brain.

While he was thinking, the soup he had been holding in his mouth had cooled and felt slimy as it slid down his throat. All the way to his gut. All the way to those neurons. All the way to that rat's brain.

Ruth

What had Ruth been reading about on her phone? Ruth had been reading about Ghost Mountain, though it was not yet known by that name. The article explained that a new mountain had appeared in a field not all that far from where Ruth and Ocho lived. The mountain had *appeared*. What did that mean, she wondered? Was it pre-existing but newly discovered? Had there been a tectonic event that forced the landscape to tent into a new peak? The article was unclear. She read it several times but was no wiser.

Ruth lifted her head to ask Ocho and found him staring at her. His face was serious and sincere. Ocho tended to overworry. It was because he was a young soul. This was a phrase her mother used to use. A young soul was different to a young person. A young soul was a soul that had lived only a few times or a few hundred times. It was still at odds with the world and found everything difficult. Everything was a problem for young souls. Their lives were full of conflict because the world was not how they would wish it to be. An old soul, on the other hand, was one that had lived many, many lives. Possibly an uncountable number of lives. It was a soul that had become attuned to the world. It had absorbed enough of the world that there was no longer a substantial difference between the world and it. This led to greater harmony. When she was a child, her mother had often said to her: "Do you know what you are, Ruth? You are an old soul." That's how Ruth heard all about young souls and old souls.

She had recently begun to ponder this dichotomy in relation to her marriage. Ocho was often difficult in small ways. He was pass-remarkable about unimportant things. He would criticise her about immaterial daily nothings. But once she understood that he had a young soul, unlike her old soul, she knew that their differences were inevitable and that it would take incalculable lifetimes to resolve them. Her acceptance of this, she thought, was a further sign that her soul was indeed old. The thought comforted her like the warm soup she swallowed, which settled in her calm stomach.

Discovery of Ghost Mountain

Ghost Mountain was discovered by a woman walking her dog. She had often taken her dog there, despite the landowner having vociferously insisted that there was no public right of way. The courts had agreed with him. The woman had argued otherwise and cited custom and practice, fair usage, common law, citizen's arrest and other abstract legal principles of uncertain status, but the judge was unmoved.

In time, the landowner died and left his land to his estranged son, who had emigrated some years before. The land was a patchwork of unconnected, uncultivated fields. "What am I supposed to do with all that?" the estranged son had asked himself. "It's a mess." Being estranged, his father's passing had left him with another mess in the form of unresolved feelings and so on. But after the argument that had led to the estrangement, the son had vowed that he would never again use metaphors, and so he refused to relate the patchwork of fields to his relationship with his father or his feelings after his father's death. Instead, he decided he would ignore the inherited land and leave it to go wild, once again resisting any metaphorical import of doing so.

As a consequence, the woman walking her dog now enjoyed a de facto public right of way, if not a de jure one, and continued to let her dog loose across the fields where he would play and empty his bladder before bounding happily home.

She was halfway up Ghost Mountain – as it would later be called – before she noticed the exacting toll on her thighs and calves. She broke off her morning reflections to check her bearings. The field was not as it had always been and her first thought was that in her preoccupation she had taken a wrong turn. Pausing to look around, she could see the road and, further on, the roof of her own house, which was not usually visible from the field.

As she stood in thought, her dog approached but without his usual playful gait. His tail was not so much wagging as swaying drunkenly. His head was lowered and instead of the usual panting satisfaction there was an unnatural quiet about him. The tennis ball he had found in a ditch was stuck in his throat.

The woman tried to reach her fingers deep into her dog's mouth but the ball was more than halfway lodged. There was no gap for her fingers to gain purchase and her initial attempts seemed to push it further down. She stood behind him and drew her clenched fists into his stomach to Heimlich the ball free, but to no effect. The dog became listless and could no longer hold himself up. In the end she sat beside him and stroked his flank as he lay there, unconscious. As a child she had lost several dogs. Her parents always told her the dogs had "gone to the country," though she had never once seen a field of dogs. This was the first dog that had died in front of her.

She had great difficulty getting the dog back to her house. It was an endeavour without dignity. She lay him on the back seat of her small car and brought him to the vet where nothing could be done.

So, it is not hard to understand why, as she lay alone in bed on that particular night, she was not thinking about what would later become known as Ghost Mountain and had told no one about it.

Hee-Haw

Ocho and Ruth lay beside each other in bed. She wore loose pyjamas and he wore boxer shorts and a vest. They had just coupled or, as they often described it, they had had "Hee-Haw."

When Ocho was a young boy, his mother had walked into his room while he was privately discovering himself. She bolted. He was left frozen in the pose she had found him in. It was one of those moments that had a feeling of repercussions about it. For some time, Ocho had been starting his day that way. It was his waking up routine. He had felt no shame about it but the incident with his mother stirred in him the understanding that shame was a question of the relationship between our own acts and other people. He was deeply ashamed over breakfast and again later when she emptied the laundry basket in his room. For her part, she feigned an imperturbable normality as a way of conveying to him that, as far as she was concerned, nothing had changed. Though she hadn't fully appreciated it herself, she was actually schooling him in the adult concept of denial. This was different to a child's concept of denial, which is about not confessing to an adult. Adult denial was about not confessing to yourself.

Later that evening, his father entered his room and sat on his bed.

"Have you been sleeping well?" he asked.

"Yes. Very well," said Ocho.

Ocho was often mystified by his father, who dressed in army fatigues, even though he was not in the military. He worked in road maintenance and often smelled of tar. He operated the Stop/Go signs at the roadworks. The reason he wore army fatigues, he said, was because they were durable, comfortable clothes and they were cheap to buy at the army surplus shop. Even when he retired years later, he still wore them. He still smelled of tar.

Ocho's father knocked on his bedroom door every evening for a few weeks to ask him if he was sleeping well. Ocho always answered that he was sleeping well but didn't mention that this was partly because he had started to discover himself at bedtime also.

With no progress, his mother came into his room one morning, after knocking, and said that his father was bringing him out to learn about nature. This, it turned out, meant the open farm where Ocho's class went every year for its school tour.

At the open farm, his father leaned his elbows on the fence at the donkey sanctuary. He had a philosophical look in his eyes.

"Donkey milk is much better than cow milk. Much higher in goodness and lower in fat. It is the most like human breast milk." He turned to Ocho. "Do you know what I mean?"

Ocho, who didn't know, said "Yes."

They waited there for quite some time. Ocho asked if he could pull some of the long grass outside the enclosure and feed it to the donkeys through the fence but his father said, "Not yet."

In time, one of the stallions mounted one of the Jennies and brayed in climax.

"You see?" said his father, mysteriously. "Hee-Haw."

Ocho nodded. "Hee-Haw."

His father said it was OK to feed the long grass to the donkey now.

Ocho told this story to Ruth after they had been dating for a while and their sex life had developed some regularity. She thought it was funny and it became part of their store of relationship in-jokes to the point where it became ordinary short hand.

That night, as Ocho and Ruth lay in bed after Hee-Haw, Ocho began to overworry again. Ruth was sleeping on her back. He lay on his back also. They had been holding each other's hands but now that she was asleep, her grip had relaxed and so it was more true to say that he was holding her hand. He knew he couldn't sleep like this but for some reason, he couldn't pick the exact moment to let go. At each moment, the moment after it seemed easier. He tried counting the moments and then counting down the moments. He fell asleep like this, but his dreams were also full of overworry. When he awoke there was a mug of coffee beside his bed and Ruth was already in the shower. When she was drying her hair in the bedroom afterwards he asked whether they were holding hands when she woke up.

Ruth thought he was joking.

The New Mountain

The death of the woman's dog left her with that feeling of displacement we call grief. She was used to the support of her neighbours on many practical matters, for example the borrowing of a ladder, but practical people can sometimes be found wanting when it comes to abstract feelings with many shades.

"I was unprepared for his absence," she said to her neighbour, the farmer, about her dog.

The farmer had been breaking up an old oil tank but stopped to listen to her.

"You could get another dog. Or cats are good – you don't have to bring them for walks." He spoke as if they were substituting swedes for turnips in a stew.

From the way he was standing with the lump hammer in his oily hands, she could see that having solved her problem, he was now keen to return to work. When his own wife had died he had been back at work on the farm the same day.

At the butcher's, she explained that she would not need a bag of liver this week or any future week and explained why. The butcher himself had two dogs and he was – either logically or counterintuitively – known throughout the town as an animal lover. He was sorry to hear that, he said, chopping a neck of pork. Not everyone understands the loss of a dog, he said, but it was always a bad loss. Sensing that she had finally found someone who understood her, she told the whole story to him as he wrapped and weighed her order and gave her the ticket so she could pay up at the front of the shop. The shop had strict rules about butchers handling meat or money but not both.

"I didn't notice at first because I was distracted by the new mountain," she said.

The butcher asked about the new mountain.

She explained and after several rounds of the butcher's questions, she was advised to report the incident. It took a moment for her to appreciate that by "incident" he meant the new mountain and not the choking of her dog. She had once again been delivered back to the world of practical people. He had already moved on to weighing mince for the next customer.

The woman's heart felt heavy, but nobody cared to weigh it.

Ocho wasn't always like this

Ruth was painting her toenails. Ocho had said that he would go outside to sit on the wall while the sun went down, and there he sat, although facing east, with the sun behind him.

Ocho wasn't always like this, thought Ruth.

She had first met him in the cinema. She had bought a ticket to see a European movie. It was a meditation on grief and loss with some sex in it. She arrived late into the dark cinema and felt around for a seat and sat down with her coat on. The opening scene of the movie was set at night, with a couple arriving at a remote cottage during a rainstorm. In the next scene, the couple were having breakfast on a sunny veranda in a way that suggested they had slept together. When the cinema lit up, Ruth could see that it was entirely empty except for the man who sat in the seat next to her. Neither acknowledged the other until after the movie. They went for coffee and she liked his confidence. He wasn't confident in a confident way. It was more that she liked that he was the type of man to go to the cinema by himself during the day. It bespoke many other things she liked.

They were the same height and though people often said that she was tall they never said that he was tall. She was not attracted to him especially, but she had been on her own for several years and was starting to grow weary from the effort it took.

Their first few meetings involved meals and felt like dates rather than real life. She began to tire of them and perhaps also of him. She had expected he would ask her to the cinema during the daytime but he never did. He kept suggesting meals and would say things like, "I mean, we're going to eat anyway, so why not eat together?"

She eventually took the initiative and asked him to come to the cinema to see another European meditation on grief and loss with some sex in it. Afterwards, they slept together in his small flat. He had confessed that he had been embarrassed because the flat was so small. It had a kitchen and bed and couch all in one room. He seemed to relax and feel accepted when Ruth said she didn't mind about the flat. Once she accepted him, he started making jokes and offering spontaneous thoughts. He told her his ambitions even though he thought she would think they were stupid. She reassured him. It turned out that his ambitions were stupid but she didn't tell him that.

Ocho also seemed insecure about Ruth meeting his parents. He said his father wore military clothes and his mother was unfathomable. Ruth met them and liked them. Afterwards, Ocho said he was glad about this but a little disappointed that they liked Ruth better than they liked him. She reassured him that parents always preferred their son's girlfriends to their sons. It was how things were.

As she painted her toenails, she reflected that yes, there were many signs that Ocho had deep insecurities and that the quality of the Ocho you got depended on how secure he felt at that particular moment. There didn't appear to be a reason for his insecurities. She had asked his mother whether he had ever been dropped on his head. Ocho's mother laughed. Ocho's father didn't laugh. Then Ruth remembered about young souls and old souls. She remembered how it was the fate of old souls to find young souls.

Ocho came in from the garden and said he was a little blind after looking at the sun and that he was going upstairs to lie down on the bean bag.

"I'll let my toes dry and then I'll bring you up some of the soup that's left. And some dipping bread," she said.

"I like the colour. Is that flesh?"

"Coral," she said.

"Is that a colour or a shade?"

"It's just what's printed on the bottle," she said.

"They give each shade a name these days, but not all shades qualify as colours, you know?"

Ruth had noticed that Ocho was often pedantic about things he didn't even care about.

"Maybe," said Ruth, concentrating on the edge of her smallest toe.

There arose a void between them.

"I'm still a bit blind," he said. "So…"

"I'll bring you some soup," she repeated without lifting up her eyes. "And some dipping bread."

Ocho wasn't always like this: II

Ocho had sat on the wall with the sun behind him, watching his shadow lengthen. He had his baseball cap on backwards so his neck didn't burn. It was nothing to do with looking cool.

For the past few days he had been feeling like he was outside himself. Like he was looking at his thoughts or looking at himself instead of being himself. As usual his thoughts went round in the big empty tumble dryer of his head without meaning anything. Only these days, instead of being inside the thoughts, he felt like a spectator.

He sat on the wall and watched his thoughts come and go. Watched them peak then sink down into the rat's brain in his gut. Watched the rat's brain pump worry chemicals around the organs jammed in there. It felt like everything was too squashed. His organs had no room. His thoughts had no room. He was hoping he would be able to understand things just enough to explain them to Ruth. All he knew was that something had shifted in the world to make him doubt himself. The basic foundations of his personality had been compromised. There was no surface evidence, but he could feel within him a fissure that was filling with worry. Worry that would work away at the thin wall of confidence that held him together.

He turned and faced the sun. It's unavoidable that a person would try and look at the sun, to see what it's like. To see if people really went blind that way. His vision soon became spotted and his eyes got uncomfortable, but he held it longer than he thought would be possible. The colour of the sun jumped around as he looked at it. It went from being a liquid orange to white with patchy black circles. He tried to blink himself back to normal but his eyes were still dazzled. He wanted to wait and watch the sun go down. It had started to feel like a stand-off between the sun and him. In the end, his eyes were not strong enough to hold the sun until it disappeared all the way beneath the horizon. By the time he turned his cap around and headed inside, the sun was already dipping behind a silhouetted mountain that he had never noticed before.

Reporting the Incident

Nobody cares, thought the woman whose dog had choked. She used to think she had true friends and neighbours, but not now. Now she thought that nobody cared. It could be because they truly didn't care or that they didn't know it was important to her or perhaps they did know but didn't want to get dragged into anything. She said this to herself, aloud. She often talked to herself. She used to call it talking to the dog.

After the butcher's, she went home and put the meat in the fridge for the next day and parcelled the rest up in freezer bags. There was so much more room in the freezer now. She opened a tin of soup for her supper and emptied it into her smallest pot. After rinsing the empty tin and putting it on the shelf for recycling, she said to her absent dog, "Andy Warhol would charge millions for that." She boiled the soup and had a little cry as she did so. When it had cooled, she took a spoonful. It was salty and creamy, just how she liked it.

She thought about her options. Reporting the incident or not reporting the incident. Whenever she didn't know what to do she always waited until after a good night's sleep. As a dog person she was an early riser and so went to bed early too. It turns out the dog had trained *her*, she said to no one. But it suited her to go to bed early. Evenings had become difficult and vast for her.

She slept with a pillow between her legs in a big bed. Her dreams were vivid but not relevant. When she awoke the next morning and first re-remembered everything, it was like her dog dying all over again. How long does this last, she wondered.

She lay in bed until it was time to report the incident. She worried that the police would admonish her for being in the field, because of the court order and everything. They would see a woman in her fifties with short hair and a checked shirt and khaki chinos who no longer looked feminine or masculine and who lived alone and who had lost a court case and whose dog had choked. They would take note of her crazy story and snigger under their breath. The whole town would find out about the new mountain and for ever more she would be known by association with it. This pained her, as she resented the mountain because it reminded her of her dog choking.

In the end, with the benefit of a night's sleep, she typed up the report herself on her computer in Times New Roman, 12 point, double spaced, and printed it on her slow inkjet printer before attaching it to a brick and throwing it through the police station window.

Town Drunk

The immediate and only suspect in the brick-throwing was the town drunk. For many months he had been throwing messages attached to bricks through the police station window. Some of the messages confessed to crimes that had or maybe hadn't been committed. Others reported theories about the town or the world. Often the messages comprised ambiguous generic wisdom, much like fortune cookies. One or two made accusations about historical figures and their writings. And there was one which was simply a receipt for a pallet of bricks – this one was counted as blank and the inclusion of a receipt inadvertent.

These incidents were reported in the local paper and had become popular.

After each brick-throwing the police would call out to the town drunk's house, which was small but immaculate. They would read him the charges as well as his rights over coffee. The town drunk would then accompany them 'downtown' which was a few streets away, where they would complete the necessary paperwork and, from time to time, lock him in a cell until the judge was ready to see him. The town drunk represented himself before the judge and seemed to like her. Some said he had a crush on her. The judge lamented that the town drunk had not made more of himself in life and usually let him off with a reprimand or a fine. Whenever given a fine, the town drunk would successfully argue that it should be paid in small amounts over a long period of time. He claimed that this was not for financial reasons, but so that he would have something to live for and so that each week when he paid the small amount, he would be reminded of his mistakes and the onus placed upon him to do better in future. The judge – who after all, had faith in human nature – acceded to these requests, for which the town drunk once thanked her by throwing a bunch of flowers attached to a brick through her office window.

On this particular morning, the town drunk had an assertive headache. He had drunk both in strength and volume the night before. He felt not only sick but weepy. It cheered him to see the police at his door. They showed him the brick and also the typed message. He set aside the message and immediately threw the brick all the way across the street where it smashed the rear windscreen of a Volvo estate belonging to the woman who lived opposite. He asked if they had another brick. They said no. He retrieved the brick and again threw it from his door all the way across the street through the Volvo window, where it landed on the parcel shelf, beside a box of tissues, now full of glass.

"Not one of my bricks," he said as he went back inside to make the coffee. "It had a nice feel to it though."

He looked at the message that had been attached, holding it with two hands as if he was reading a book. He read it all the way to the end and then went back to the bits that hadn't made sense to him.

"Not one of mine either," he repeated.

The police looked at one another. "Are you sure?" they asked.

The woman who owned the Volvo came across the street, still pulling the arm of her cardigan on. What she had to say was declarative and vituperative. The town drunk offered to pay for the Volvo window in small amounts over time, explaining what he would learn from this. He also clarified that it was not his brick though he did throw it.

The woman went back to her house, muttering oaths.

"You know, she used to peer through my front window whenever she passed by my house," the town drunk said after she had left. "So, I decided to wait for her one time, and when she looked in, I was standing in my underpants waving out to her."

After the police had left, he sat by himself and thought about what the note had said about a new mountain and how, on reading it, the weepy feeling in his stomach had melted away.

Carthage and Clare

Ocho and Ruth were invited to dinner at the house of Carthage and Clare. They had got to know Carthage and Clare through mutual friends they no longer saw. It used to be that the mutual friends, Ocho and Ruth, and Carthage and Clare would meet for dinner, but after the mutual friends had children, they started cancelling, so eventually the arrangement shrank to the two couples.

"You should make more of an effort to see your friends," Ruth would say to Ocho.

"It's important to keep in touch," Clare would say to Carthage.

"But he's not really my friend," Ocho and Carthage would reply to their respective wives.

And so they kept meeting.

As they waited for the food, Carthage said things to Ocho like, "Who do you know in Company X? Do you know Mr Y in Company X? I've known Mr Y in Company X for ages. A good guy, a good guy ..."

Ocho didn't like the way Carthage related to people as if they were at work. It was as though Ocho were a fridge magnet and Carthage was trying to work out whether to place him at eye level with the important magnets, or nearer the bottom with the other magnets you never looked at.

He also didn't like the way things were between Carthage and Ruth. Because Ocho and Ruth were the same height, and she wore heels when they went out, she was taller than him, as was Carthage, who was in turn taller than Ruth. When it was the three of them together, Ocho, the shortest, felt like

Carthage and Ruth were the father and mother and he was the child. From this, he had got the idea that there was something between Carthage and Ruth. Once the idea of there being something between them became established in Ocho's mind, he saw confirmation in everything, no matter how innocent. If Carthage was looking at Ruth when he said, "So good to see you both again" or if he complimented them on the gifts they'd brought – which Ruth had chosen – Ocho would feel depressed.

Ocho left Ruth and Carthage chatting and followed Clare into the kitchen. He stood in the kitchen doorway and watched her as she stacked the dishwasher and laid out teacups and finger-sized cake slices on a tray. He asked himself how he would feel if this was his life and if Clare was doing this in a kitchen they shared together. Ocho offered to help and asked Clare how her job was going, though he couldn't remember what she did. She smiled in an unrevealing way and said, "Usual schmusual."

He was intimidated by her reservedness, which made her unfathomable to him.

She handed him the tray to bring into the other room and with the gentlest of pressure on his elbow, set him turning around and off back to the others. Could he spend his life with someone who would simply point him in a direction and set him off like that?

Ruth and Carthage were leaning forward in excited conversation as Ocho set down the tea things. He poured for them and passed them the fingers of cake. All this made him feel invisible, like a stagehand. Made him feel worthless, like a magnet at the bottom of the fridge door.

They were talking about what would become known as Ghost Mountain. The story had begun to obsess the whole town and had broken through to the national news cycle. Everyone was talking about how a new mountain had been discovered by the town drunk. The local newspaper that first broke the story knew the town drunk had been eliminated from inquiries, but all its most popular stories included him – for whatever reason people liked to know what he got up to – so they cast him in the lead role. From a newsworthiness point of view, it had worked well, as the appeal of the story was in something happening with the right balance of plausibility and implausibility. In other words, it was a story that gave people something to think about.

"It is clearly tectonic-related," suggested Ruth. "I mean, nobody alive has ever witnessed the birth of any of the other mountains in the world, so we don't know, experientially-speaking, how they arrive. We only have reasonable theories that must now be revisited."

"Yes, that's true. I hadn't thought of that," said Carthage.

Ocho saw this as another example of there being something between Carthage and Ruth. Carthage always liked to have the last word in arguments. There was no way he would agree with something so stupid unless he was in love, or at least thinking of Hee-Haw.

"The mountain was always there," interrupted Ocho. "It's small-town opportunism – drumming-up a novelty to generate tourism. Surely there are official sources that can establish the facts, but the town—"

"—You wouldn't say that if this happened in a city," interrupted Clare, as she joined them at the table. "Small towns are often the birthplace of great scientists and political leaders," she continued, addressing Carthage and Ruth, but not Ocho, "whereas most criminals come from cities."

"Very true, very true," said Carthage and Ruth as they poured milk for each other.

Ocho had put the cake finger in his mouth without realizing that it still had its translucent baking paper casing. In the moment's silence that followed Clare's insight, he had to spit the paper into a cloth napkin with the others watching him.

He felt like he had disgusted everyone.

Ordnance Survey

The police had leaked the story about the new mountain to the local paper as a way of flushing out leads.

At that point they had not yet been authorized to visit the so-called new mountain. They had been instructed to refer to it as "so-called" until the facts were established. In the absence of a crime scene or an official charge, they were not minded to open a formal case file on the grounds of curiosity alone. In any event, with the estranged son, now landowner, overseas, the case would involve international cooperation with possible treaty implications. The paperwork alone would give rise to a second new mountain, said one officer. He repeated the line to his wife later that evening, making her proud.

The ordnance survey office had one desk with a computer, a phone, some stationery, a photocopier and a special storage cabinet full of maps. There was also just enough room for the man who worked there, known as the Clerk of Maps. The police arrived at his small office looking to establish, scientifically speaking, whether the mountain was new or not. Surely the definitive record of any pre-existing mountain would be held by the Clerk of Maps at the ordnance survey office.

The Clerk of Maps tried not to smile as he listened to the police. He couldn't help them, he said, and then clarified that he *wanted* to help them but was unable to do so. He was leaning back in his chair with his fingers interlocked and his thumbs circling each other.

"Why not?" they asked.

"Well..."

The pause was so important. It was the culmination of his career frustrations and his stilted initiative and his stunted professional conscientiousness and his unheeded warnings.

"...the local maps don't show elevation," he said.

The Clerk of Maps had entered a career in ordnance survey because he liked the outdoors and was fascinated by the untold story of the landscape. After many years as a Junior Clerk of Maps, he was selected for a Government-sponsored ordnance survey scholarship programme during which he shook the hand of the Chief Surveyor who congratulated him on his fine draughtsmanship. He was later appointed Clerk of Maps on promotion, albeit in an acting capacity.

The promotion gave him the confidence to persuade his wife to transfer with him to a small town she had never heard of, where he promised they would build their future and make the babies she was so keen to bring into the world.

But his promotion was to be a disappointment. His main duty turned out to be making copies of local maps for people involved in boundary disputes. The job was well-paid and secure but he was unhappy because his skills were unused and the maps he had brought with him remained unpacked, as did his theodolite.

On his arrival, he had disparaged the level of detail on the local maps, which showed boundaries but not elevations. His first priority as new Acting Clerk of Maps, he told his superiors, would be to bring the local maps up to what he considered a baseline level of ordnance survey detail. Anything less would be tantamount to negligence and philistinism, he had said in his first report as Acting Clerk of Maps. He had wanted to reassure them that his arrival would restore the degraded dignity of their profession.

But his superiors' reaction was concise and unambiguous: "Don't make waves."

After receiving their response, he returned home to his wife, where it took him a broken night's sleep before he could explain

28

to her what had happened. The more he discussed it, the more he peeled back the layers of meaning it contained. He was not, after all, being groomed for greater things. He realised that he had been given a minor assignment in the middle of nowhere because, in their assessment, it was all he could be trusted with. His acting status was simply a lure, a dummy reward that he had fallen for. And, saddest of all, he now came to see the failure of his career as part of a more general failure. So far there had been no baby and the doctors had advised him and his wife not to expect one.

But the arrival of the police into his office was to be a great day for him. A vindication. He had already read the newspaper reports about the new mountain and he had held his peace as his neighbours made small talk about how he must know a lot about mountains, what with him being a geologist (he wasn't). He had also fielded many calls to his office from people looking for a photograph of the new mountain. He told them politely that he didn't photograph mountains and that the instrument they were probably thinking of was called a theodolite. He resisted adding that there was no 'i' in ordnance.

Listening to the police in this small office, he realised he had on his hands potentially the biggest "I told you so" in the town's ordnance survey history. Deep inside himself he said the words "glorious" and "delicious."

He drove straight home at lunchtime and made passionate love to his wife. It was the beginning of a beautiful summer of many such lunchtimes for them.

Naming the Mountain

There were conflicting stories about the circumstances surrounding the discovery of the mountain and the exact status of its newness remained a matter of dispute. Also, in those early days, it didn't yet have an official name, though it had many unofficial names.

The police referred to it as the "so-called" new mountain.

The woman who had first discovered it – and whose dog had choked there – named it after her dog and referred to it as Thelonious Mountain.

The town drunk referred to it as Brick-Throwing Mountain.

The Clerk of Maps and his wife both referred to it as Lunchtime Mountain.

The butcher thought of it as Choking Dog Mountain, but as an animal lover, and out of sensitivity towards the poor woman who had lost her pet and companion, he took care never to speak about it that way.

Clare simply referred to it as New Mountain.

Carthage, who, according to Ocho, was trying to be poetic to impress Ruth, called it Suddenly Mountain.

In response, Ocho referred to it, in his own head at least, as Stupid Dick Mountain.

Ruth, who spoke of little else around the house, referred to it as Spirit Mountain.

The town authorities gave careful consideration to the options. They understood the wisdom of desire lines.

In times past, when the local authorities built a new public park, they would lay a path across it to encourage people to stay off the grass. But the public, with an intuitive group wisdom, would elect their own preferred route and new parks would end up with two paths: the official, paved path, and a second, dirt path worn into the grass – the desire line. The town authorities had therefore learned to defer to this form of popular wisdom and so, over time, they stopped paving paths on new parks. Instead, they would wait until the public had cut their own desire line, and then they would pave over that.

This was the wisdom of desire lines.

They took the same approach with naming the mountain. In time, people began to make the journey out of town to see it for themselves. There was no direct access from the road and so it was necessary to park some distance away and approach it across the patchwork of fields owned by the overseas landowner who had inherited the land from his estranged father. From this viewpoint, there appeared to be two hollows sitting like sunken sockets about halfway up its slope. A third hollow lay between but below the first two, creating what looked like a haunted expression.

And that was how it came to be known as Ghost Mountain by everyone who saw it.

Theodolite

The town drunk was assisting the Clerk of Maps on Ghost Mountain. The police had suggested him to the Clerk of Maps owing to his amenable nature and copious free time. But because his hands shook, he was not suited to surveying, so instead his main job that day was to stop people interrupting the Clerk of Maps. He had an assertive headache that morning and the fresh air did him good.

If people came up and asked to have their picture taken with the mountain he would explain that the instrument was a theodolite. For most people this was a new word in that it was new to them. The town drunk would say that it was a new word for him also. He intuitively understood the need to find something in common. He was also self-deprecating and joked that he was only there to carry the theodolite back to the car in case the Clerk of Maps got struck by lightning. The town drunk made this joke throughout the morning.

At midday, the Clerk of Maps said that he was going to spend his lunchtime at home. The town drunk offered to share his own packed lunch, but the Clerk of Maps said he had already eaten while the town drunk had been joking with the walkers.

Once the Clerk of Maps had left, the town drunk sought a suitable spot on the side of the mountain where he could empty his bladder. He walked around clockwise and soon began to ponder how Ghost Mountain looked different with each step and that he too – in a way – was also different, and how that could lead to an infinite number of possibilities. But his bladder was full, so he broke off that thought on noticing his own urgency. Of course, there is no such thing as the front and back of a mountain, so it was not like the church where he had often snuck around to the rear when he needed to go. There was also part of him that wanted to do it off the top of the mountain. To be the first to do that, at least as far as he knew. In the end, he chose a spot on the leeward side and arched his stream into the air with the mountain behind him. When doing his business outside he was often fascinated by the effect the wind had.

When he returned to the windward side, there was a woman inspecting the theodolite. He wiped his wet fingertips on his trousers and approached her.

"It's been a long time since I've seen a theodolite up close," she said.

This impressed the town drunk more than he could say.

"I'm not a surveyor," he said. "I'm helping the Clerk of Maps."

"I know. I've seen you around. You're the town alcoholic. You're always in the papers."

"I'm not an alcoholic," he said.

"Oh, I'm sorry. I thought that was common knowledge."

"I'm the town drunk. That's different."

"What's the difference?"

"I enjoy getting drunk and being drunk, but I'm not addicted."

He saw that she might know what a theodolite was but that she didn't know the difference between a drunk and an alcoholic. Still, he was hugely impressed by her.

"I can see how it's confusing," he said. "Think of it this way: the town carpenter does carpentry but he's not addicted to it."

"But that's a job," she said. "Being a drunk is not a job."

He thought for a moment. It was so much easier to enjoy a conversation now his bladder was at rest.

"You're right: it's not a job, but it is a *role*."

He could see that she was considering this. She was neither pedantic nor argumentative. That also impressed him.

"I was about to have lunch. Would you like to join me?" he asked.

"What are you having?"

"Tinned tuna, nuts and apples."

"No bread?"

"Well, some bread too. That goes without saying."

"Are you going to drink alcohol?"

"I'm not going to lie to you. I have a small bottle of red wine. Enough for a big glass or two smaller glasses if you'd like to share?"

"I'm not drinking at the moment. I'm in mourning."

"I'm sorry to hear that," he said. "Who died?"

"My dog choked on a tennis ball here. I was the first to discover the mountain, though I've read that you're taking the credit for that."

So, it was her brick, he thought. He was impressed yet again.

"That's the problem with newspapers," he said. "They print lies. I told the police it wasn't me who discovered the mountain."

She sat on the side of the mountain and looked over the flat, unremarkable fields. The wind was blowing a Mexican wave in the grass.

"I could tell the police that it was you, if you like. I could tell the newspaper too – they know me well, so it wouldn't be any trouble."

"It's OK," she said. "I'm not actually supposed to be here. There's a Court Order against me."

The town drunk took his lunch out of his bag. All except the wine.

"I see," he said. "You're the lady from the Court case."

"That's me. Also, I don't want to get into trouble over the police station window."

She lifted a thermos flask from her bag on the grass.

"Would you like some soup?" she offered.

"Is it salty," he asked. "Or creamy?"

"Both," she said.

"No thanks."

He was still a little dehydrated from his hangover.

"What was your dog's name?" he asked.

"Thelonious," she answered.

It sounds a little like theodolite, he thought, but didn't say so, as it was sort of the same but still quite different.

Chicken

"Do you think there could be some non-geological explanation?" asked Ruth.

She was reading about Ghost Mountain on her phone again, while sitting-leaning on the washing machine. Ocho was on the back step using cotton buds to clean dog dirt from the treads on the soles of his old shoes. He paused to answer her.

"I think it's probably nothing," he said.

"I mean like a spiritual explanation. Like it's a message or a sign?"

Ocho started cleaning his shoes again. He didn't want to play at this whatever-it-was.

"Aren't you interested?" she asked.

"I think the fact that I'd rather clean dog shit is a message or a sign."

"You're so coarse. Why are you always so coarse?"

Ruth went back to reading her phone. He could hear her typing something.

"You can turn off that tick-tick typing noise, you know. It's in 'Settings.'"

Ruth continued typing. Then her phone rang.

"Oh, I wasn't expecting you to ring back," she said in a smiling voice. "I was only checking if you'd seen it."

Her voice faded as she moved to the next room.

"Dog shit Carthage," said Ocho to nobody.

He washed his hands and left his shoes out on the step. He hadn't done a thorough job so they were still too dirty to wear. He left them soles-up – maybe the rain would clean them.

36

He had arranged to call over to see his parents. He preferred to see them on a midweek evening – that way it would be a short visit. It was better if he told them he was dropping something off, so it was more like an errand, meaning he didn't have to bring Ruth. If they visited at the weekend, they would both have to stay for dinner and then for the whole afternoon. His parents would coo over Ruth and she would get them all excited about Ghost Mountain. He wanted to get to them first and tell them Ghost Mountain was stupid. His parents were suggestible. They often adopted the views of other people. He knew they would have followed the news stories and would buy into the whole thing. But if he told them it was stupid they would be influenced by that. They thought that as Ocho was younger he came from the real world, whereas they were older so only got their news second hand. They had been like that since they had retired.

Having told his parents he had something to drop off, he now needed cover for his story. He went to the butcher's. He would tell his parents that he and Ruth had bought two chickens by mistake and that the second chicken would go off before it got eaten, so they could have it. His parents would suggest that Ocho should keep and freeze it, so he would need a lie about their freezer being full. He lied to his parents all the time, especially about unimportant things. It had become a habit.

The butcher started small talk about Ghost Mountain. Something about a dog being killed there or something.

"Probably Satanists," said Ocho.

He gave his parents the chicken and explained the whole thing. They asked him why he didn't freeze it, so he was ready for that too. His father was wearing a khaki t-shirt that was a little too large for him. It seemed like he had lost weight.

His mother looked pale.

"Are you OK?" he asked as he kissed her forehead.

"I'm tired, that's all."

"I keep telling her to rest more. Sit down. Read a book or something. But she buzzes around like a bluebottle all day," said his father.

"I like to keep busy," she protested gently.

His mother had made him some chicken stew. Seemed like they already had plenty of chicken. He sat at the kitchen table and they sat opposite him. His parents weren't eating so they watched him eat. With anyone else it would have felt strange but not with his parents. It was nice to be their favourite when Ruth wasn't there.

"How is Ruth?" asked his mother. "We haven't seen her in a while."

"Well, she's OK. All caught up in this stupid Ghost Mountain story."

"Don't you believe the story?" asked his father. "We were wondering about it and we both said – didn't we – that we wondered what you thought of it."

"Unfortunately, I heard there are Satanists killing dogs up there now."

His mother covered her mouth with her hand.

"I suppose, that's what you get with Satanists," said his father. "That's what gives them a bad name. Have you been up there yet?"

"Me? No. I didn't think anyone was allowed. It's on private land. And anyway, it's all nothing. Mountains are a geological phenomenon. That stuff doesn't happen overnight."

"Well, it could have been tectonic," suggested his father. "Have the scientists tested it? The news stories don't tell you anything. I expect it's all cordoned off and scientists are working up there."

"You're assuming that it's a new mountain," said Ocho. "If there are no scientists up there, that tells you all you need to know."

"We were thinking of going this weekend," said his mother. "But maybe it's a bad idea. What do you think?"

"It's a free country," said Ocho, tipping the last of the stew into his mouth from the bowl directly. "But you won't find me picnicking up there with Satanists, that's for sure."

When Ocho arrived home, Ruth was already dozing in bed. Ocho got in beside her, hopeful of Hee-Haw but then Ruth said she had brought his shoes in from outside in case they got rained on. The thought of dog shit made him think of Carthage and the mood was broken.

As Ruth breathed calmly beside him, Ocho lay awake with his arms above the sheets, his mind full of Carthage and his body full of chicken stew.

Visiting Ghost Mountain

More and more people began to venture out to see Ghost Mountain for themselves. As they approached, many would comment that they could see how it got its name. Being a new mountain, there was no path to the top, so most people tended to stay at the foot of it. Looking towards its crest, they would observe that it was smaller than they had expected. Some queried whether it was more of a large hill, but no, most people said it was definitely a mountain, without being specific about how that was defined. They supposed you could measure its height in contrast to the surrounding landscape, which was largely flat and unremarkable. They also suggested that you could measure its height above sea level, but being so far inland, that would not tell you much. How would a person even visualise that? By that measure the flat fields around them could be considered mountains.

Someone decided to walk around Ghost Mountain. They could have gone anti-clockwise, but for some reason clockwise felt more natural. As they walked, they noticed something slightly new about the mountain with each step. Having completed a circuit, you could say they had seen as many mountains as they had taken steps. The difference was subtle. You could say it was as subtle as the 'b' in subtle. But not only was Ghost Mountain different with each step, so too was the person who walked around it. With each step they absorbed something new and this something new changed them in subtle ways.

This experience was felt by many people who walked around Ghost Mountain.

It was felt by people who were walking with no intention of thinking about these things.

It was felt by people who always overthought things.

It was felt by people who were trying to be interesting.

It was felt by people who didn't want to be there in the first place.

And so it happened that many people who visited Ghost Mountain began to circle around it in this way and with that experience. Of course, some people immediately started to scale up Ghost Mountain, which was not difficult, as it was limpet-shaped and not particularly high. Others went back to their cars without seeing what the fuss was about. And, inevitably, some people walked around it in an anti-clockwise direction. But generally, people fell into walking around it the same way. Even those who arrived when Ghost Mountain was deserted and who knew nothing about its circumnavigation would find themselves doing the same thing as the people before them had done.

No Longer Acting

The Clerk of Maps had been made substantive in his role. The qualifier 'Acting' was removed from all official correspondence. The new maps he had produced, showing the contour lines at Ghost Mountain, were being printed, and there was talk of him delivering a paper to his superiors, who were open to including contour lines on a wider range of maps, especially those considered as possible sites for future mountains. He scoffed at their opportunism while still feeling gratified by the recognition they granted him. This was how it worked when an I-told-you-so corrupted a person. It started by repairing his hurt feelings, but then became like a bird pecking his mind. When other people said something stupid, the pecking bird would whisper that what they said was stupid. Whenever he did something useful – even if it was part of his job and therefore something he was paid to do – the pecking bird would tell him that only he could have done it or done it so well. Most of all, the pecking bird would congratulate him on how grounded and modest he had been about the whole thing, remarking on how others might have handled it differently. In this way, the pecking bird, whose voice spoke softly and sympathetically in his brain, befriended him.

During those hot carnal foodless lunchtimes with his wife, he would notice her noticing how he had changed. He would notice her noticing his energy and creativity, his daring and his tenderness. And afterwards he would hold her and she would rest quietly beside him with her hand on his chest. The evidence of his transformation was undisputed. He could see now that the meandering way in which he had wandered through life was in fact an apprenticeship of disappointment that was necessary to teach him to recognise true happiness when it eventually arrived.

He had a little time left before he had to peel his sweaty body from his wife's side and return to the office. As he lay there, he listened to the pecking bird that was his friend. He listened and delighted in what it told him.

Overseas Landowner

The new overseas landowner of Ghost Mountain sat at his desk, eating a sandwich he had bought from his savings. What he often thought of as his savings was actually the limited spare capacity on his credit card. He was in his twenties and worked in an entry-level position at a firm that had often been mentioned in the news for either the right or the wrong reasons. His job was technical in nature and anyone with his level of education could do it. He was eminently replaceable and his terms and conditions of employment reflected this. He shared a house with three other people, none of whom were known to him before he moved in. The politics of living with strangers exhausted him.

He had been estranged from his father for a number of years. The first he learned of his father's death was the arrival of a letter from the executrix of his father's estate advising him that he had inherited a patchwork of land.

The cause of the estrangement had been a flashpoint. When he found himself in that flashpoint with his father he had used a metaphor. It was the combination of the flashpoint and the metaphor that had truly caused the estrangement. Perhaps the estrangement was the culmination of a lifetime's worth of flashpoints and metaphors. He reflected that with his father now dead and with no other surviving family members, the reasons for the estrangement were no longer worth understanding, though he continued to ponder them.

The letter from the executrix to his father's estate had made him a landowner. This was strange because until that point, he had never been wealthy or even particularly well-paid. He didn't feel like he thought a landowner would feel. "Am I rich now?" he asked himself. As he sat on the old couch with a housemate he didn't know, watching the housemate play video games, he thought "Am I rich now?" At a meeting where he had one irrelevant question his boss had instructed him to raise, he was distracted by the thought, "Am I rich now?"

He also asked himself, "Does this mean my father still loved me?" But no sooner had he considered that thought than another thought succeeded it: "Does this mean my father still hated me?"

The whole thing was a mess.

A second letter had arrived saying that the people of the town were breaching the recent Court order secured by his father. The Court had established that there was no public right of way, and yet people continued to walk across his land to see the new mountain. "Please advise," requested the letter.

"What new mountain?" he thought. "What *is* a new mountain?"

That evening, he bought some cheap wine and a bag of chocolate raisins using his credit card savings. In his room, he removed his shoes and lay on the bed, still wearing his suit.

One of his housemates slipped a note under his door with a grievance on it.

Looking for a flashpoint.

Happy Birthday!

Ocho never knew what to buy his father for his birthday. He suspected he didn't know his father that well.

"What does he like?" Ruth asked him.

Ocho thought about his father. He had never thought about him as a person. As a human. He had only thought of him as his father, whatever that meant. To Ocho, a father was merely a man in his life who didn't do or say much. Ocho treated his father as if he were a robot who only came to life when Ocho entered the room and who went limp again after he left. He never considered what his father got up to when he wasn't around.

"He likes clothes, I think?" said Ocho.

"Are you sure? Doesn't he always wear army clothes?"

Ocho thought that because his father always wore army clothes that he must like them a lot. But something about Ruth's reaction now told him that this was the wrong thing to think.

"Maybe I could buy him a book?" he said.

"What does he read?"

Ocho thought about the bookshelf in his parents' house. He couldn't recall the names of any of the books, or whether the books belonged to his mother or his father. He suspected that if either of them read it was more likely to be his mother. He didn't want to buy a book as it meant he would have to read it first. It seemed like a lot of work. He would have to make sure there was nothing unusual or unfathomable in it. He would have to make sure it was free from Hee-Haw.

"We could get him a nice bottle of wine. Or whiskey maybe?" Ruth suggested.

Ocho had only seen his father drunk once. It was on a boat, so it was hard to tell whether it was the motion that made him susceptible to drunkenness. His father had put his arm around him and said all sort of things Ocho couldn't make out. Ocho didn't learn anything about his father from the experience.

When they called over to the house that weekend, Ruth wore a pretty dress with cornflowers on it. She wore heels, which meant she would be the tallest one at the birthday celebration. Ocho's parents were not tall and seemed to be getting smaller.

In the end, Ocho was too paralysed by indecision, so Ruth picked the present for his father. She bought him some aftershave. It came in a white cube and the label said it had notes of leather, tobacco and figs. Ocho joked that it would make his father smell like a sailor. He made the same joke again when Ruth gave his father the present and bent down to kiss him on the cheek. His father sprayed the aftershave onto his chin but accidentally sprayed some into his mouth. He coughed a little but was clearly moved by the present. He was used to smelling like tar from his job, but now he smelled like the President, he said.

Ruth also brought flowers for Ocho's mother.

Ocho's mother had bought her husband a new belt for his birthday.

"He's lost weight," she said.

"You look tired," said Ocho to his mother.

"Let me help you in the kitchen," said Ruth.

Ocho sat with his father in the front room. His father was wearing his new belt and his new aftershave. Ocho could smell his father. He could smell the aftershave but also the tar.

Ocho's mother and Ruth were laughing together when they entered the room and broke the silence.

"He'll never change …" was the last thing he heard his mother say, which made Ruth laugh.

His father had a glass of milk with his meal. Ocho and Ruth had wine. Ocho's mother drank tea – she said the wine would make her sleepy.

Afterwards they all stood in the kitchen together. Ocho's parents cleaned up right after a meal. They always did it together. Ruth was helping them. Ocho stood to the side. He was helping by not getting in their way.

His parents looked small beside Ruth. Whenever she spoke, they stopped what they were doing and looked up at her. To Ocho, it looked like the words were pouring out of Ruth's mouth and into his parents' brains.

They talked about Ghost Mountain.

Ocho's parents asked Ruth about the Satanists.

Ruth thought they were joking. She asked Ocho whether he had heard about them.

Ocho said he had heard about a dog. The butcher had told him. The butcher was an animal lover.

Ruth said the butcher killed animals – did that make him a Satanist?

Ocho's parents looked at him. Their brains were full of what Ruth had just said. They looked to him to replace it with something else.

"Don't look at me. I haven't been there. I'm only telling you what I heard."

His parents looked up at Ruth again. Ruth said she believed in mountains but she didn't believe in Satanists. For a moment Ocho's parents didn't know how to react, but when Ruth laughed they laughed too. They seemed so relieved.

In the car on the way home, they got held up at the level crossing for the crosstown train. Ruth said Carthage had suggested that they all go up to Ghost Mountain together. It would be fun, he had said, and now Ruth said the same thing.

"These barriers come down way too early," said Ocho as there was still no sign of the train. "The whole thing is so stupid."

"Well, I'm going," said Ruth.

Boots

Ocho sat at his computer at home, working and wearing his new boots. It was the first pair of boots he had ever bought or worn. He bought them because he didn't want to clean the dog dirt from his old shoes anymore. He was wearing the boots around the house to break them in, which made his feet throb every day. He bought circular plasters for his heels and plaster strips for his big toe and little toe. But the boots worked through the plasters and his feet hurt anyway. All day as he worked he thought only of his feet. And Ghost Mountain. Though he was pointedly not talking about Ghost Mountain. He wanted to show the world, meaning Ruth, that he was not part of the Ghost Mountain stupidity.

Ruth was on the phone with Carthage upstairs in the bedroom. She had brought the phone up there after answering it. Ocho's attention followed her upstairs and his imagination floated in the bedroom above her as she talked and listened. His body stayed downstairs, stuck in his boots. His feet hurt so much.

Ocho couldn't concentrate on his computer screen.

Ocho wanted to go upstairs but his feet hurt so much.

His rat's brain saw him wanting a coffee purely so that he could walk upstairs and ask Ruth if she wanted a coffee too. His rat's brain saw his intentions. His rat's brain saw the selfishness in everything.

Ocho walked upstairs slowly and painfully, like a defeated army. He usually clambered upstairs, more or less on all fours, using his hands on the steps ahead. Ruth only ever walked the

49

stairs upright. She would have been able to climb the stairs balancing a glass of water on her head without spilling it, whereas he scampered like a dog.

Walking up the stairs rubbed his boots differently against his feet, making them pinch in new ways.

In the bedroom, Ruth was on a call using headphones. Ocho couldn't hear the other voice. Her glasses were on the bed. He had often warned her not to leave her glasses on the bed. They would get broken. She didn't have a spare pair. She needed her glasses. And they were expensive. She should be more careful of them.

Ruth didn't look up when he moved her glasses to the bedside table.

Ocho caught her eye and made a C symbol with his fingers. This meant coffee, though it also now reminded him of Carthage. She waved in a way that said she didn't want any, thanks.

Ocho went back downstairs and made a cup of coffee that he didn't want either. He saw it through so as to be seen to see it through. Seeing things through was his way of making a liar of his rat's brain. Like he did with his boots. Like he wanted to do with Carthage.

Butcher

Ruth queued at the butcher shop. She was buying meat for the picnic. They were going to Ghost Mountain that weekend with Carthage and Clare.

The man at the front of the queue was the town drunk, who she recognised from the local newspaper. He talked a lot but wasn't buying much. Ruth guessed he lived alone. He ordered small portions of a few things. He ordered food that came from pigs, cows, sheep and chickens. He ordered food that used to be pigs, cows, sheep and chickens. Ruth had to strain to hear what he was saying because of the radio that was playing in the back of the shop. The town drunk said he had been on Ghost Mountain. That he had met the woman who discovered it. The butcher said he knew the woman he was talking about. Her dog had choked on a tennis ball. Always sad to lose a dog, he said. He handed the town drunk a ticket, which had blood on it, and asked him to pay at the front of the shop.

Ruth wished she had been second in the queue so that she could have joined in the conversation.

She would have asked the town drunk what Ghost Mountain was really like and about the woman who had discovered it.

She would have asked the butcher whether it was the same dog that the Satanists were supposed to have killed.

The woman in front of her had a distinctive aura. Her corkscrew curls spilled from under an olive beret. She ordered a few slices of cooked ham. The butcher had to ask someone else to get this from the fridge. His hands were for raw meat. He had blood stained into the grain of his knuckles and the sides of his nails. While they waited, he asked her about Ghost Mountain. The woman said, no, she hadn't been. Her husband had been up there with his theodolite. He was the Clerk of Maps. The butcher repeated the word theodolite. Ruth made a mental note to look up the word later.

Ruth wondered whether the butcher was an animal lover.

She wondered whether being a butcher made him a bad person.

She wondered whether you had to be an old soul to be a butcher. An old soul could live with contradictions, whereas a young soul couldn't. A young soul needed people to be all good or all bad whereas an old soul knew everyone was a mix of good and bad. An old soul knew that the mystery of life was the coexistence of good and bad within a person.

By the time it was Ruth's turn she had already been thinking too much about Ghost Mountain and the butcher. She stammered as she tried to remember her order. The butcher was calm and listened. He seemed solid to her. He seemed like an even older soul than she was. She liked being the younger soul for a change.

There was blood on the ticket he handed her with her order. After she had paid, she swiped the bloody ticket from the counter and held it in her pocket all the way home.

Headquarters Conference

The Clerk of Maps had been invited to address the Headquarters Conference on the subject of Ghost Mountain. He was asked to keep his presentation short and light, and to include local colour. The mapping of a small mountain was not in itself an innovation, but nevertheless people were curious. He kissed his wife before he left and promised they would do something nice with the travel and subsistence money he would earn.

At the conference he felt nervous and shy. He didn't know anyone and didn't recognise any of the names on the badges people wore. He opened his midday presentation by saying that he was well aware that he was the only thing standing between people and their lunch. It was customary to say such things. His presentation started with the technical business of mapping a new mountain before moving on to a non-technical account of what was happening at Ghost Mountain and the whole business of people walking around it. He ended with an impassioned plea to include elevation on a wider range of maps. The Q&A session was meant to be short, but hands shot up around the room and the roving mics were sensationally busy, right into lunchtime. The questions were all about Ghost Mountain rather than mapping.

Did he think it was a ghost?

Is it true that there were Satanists on the mountain?

Are the people who walk around the mountain members of a cult?

When will the next mountain appear?

The Clerk of Maps was charming and witty in his replies. The pecking bird told him it was all going extremely well. Many people spoke to him afterwards, and one man shook his wet hand while they were queuing for the hand dryers in the bathroom. Over lunch, a young woman from headquarters who was new to mapping sat beside him. She didn't know anybody, she said, and she found these sorts of events difficult. He told her he was the same. She was astonished to know that he had been in her position that very morning, but now he was the star of the conference.

That evening, they sat together again over dinner, and she told him that she had left teaching to get into mapping and asked him what he liked about mapping. They discussed books they enjoyed and he gave her advice about buying her first theodolite. Throughout the evening, people introduced themselves to him and asked him further questions about Ghost Mountain. He kept recycling the line that he hoped the mountain wasn't gone when he got back, or else he would have nothing to talk about next year. The young woman said she was impressed at how effortlessly he handled everything. She said she wished she was more like that. Or, as he heard it, more like *him*.

At the end of the evening, they shared a lift upstairs. When it came to her floor, he wished her a good night. He said he would look out for her at breakfast. She smiled and thanked him for the advice about the theodolite.

As the lift cranked its way up to his floor he purred with satisfaction at how well everything had gone. He was a little drunk, but only drunk enough to be merry. He was enjoying the voice of the pecking bird, which said he could have slept with the young woman had he wanted to. He enjoyed how it stoked his sense of virtue at not sleeping with her. The pecking bird told him how authentic he was.

He called his wife much later than he had promised. He apologised but explained all about his successful day and his line about hoping the mountain was still there when he got back. She was sleepy. She had left the phone on her pillow as she dozed, so as not to miss his call.

He told her not to worry. There was a charming young woman he had spent most of the evening talking to. He assured his wife that, though he could have slept with the young woman, he didn't. He wanted his wife to know what type of man he was. But his wife was silent at the other end.

Now she knew *all* about what type of man her husband was.

Crushes

The town drunk was prone to crushes. He had always been like that, owing to his romantic nature. He was not sure whether he drank to arouse his romantic nature, or whether his romantic nature caused him to drink, though he had been romantic from an early age. He first noticed it when he fell in love with his older brother's girlfriend, Mary Watchford. She had corkscrew curls, oversized glasses and a gentle face. He was still in primary school. She worked as a proofreader and once brought him to the zoo by herself, without his brother. They rode on the zoo train but the train ran over the legs of a small boy. They never found out what happened to the boy, but Mary Watchford bought iced fingers to help them get over the trauma of seeing the accident.

He was heartbroken when his older brother split up with Mary Watchford, and didn't understand why this meant he had to break up with her too. He called to her house one evening and asked if they could still be friends, but she simply kissed his hair and cried and said that's not how things worked. She gave him a keyring, but he was still young and had no keys to put on it. He never saw her again. Or he did, but much later. She came to his mother's funeral over thirty years later. It was such a nice thing to do. But that was just like Mary Watchford.

The town drunk had had many crushes over the years. He sometimes thought that the only true love he had ever experienced was his crushes. They were perfectly tragic and romantic. He couldn't work out whether he had one crush in his life, which shifted, like a spotlight, from one crush object to the next, or whether each crush was new and original. It didn't matter to him. They were all beautiful and special and he could never rank or compare them. Except maybe Mary Watchford, who was the first and the best.

Seeing the Clerk of Maps disappear every lunchtime with such happiness, only to return with even greater happiness, naturally aroused curiosity in the town drunk about the Clerk of Maps' wife, who was said to have enchanting corkscrew curls. Naturally, this reminded the town drunk of Mary Watchford, which was enough for him to construct the foundations of a new crush. Being a man of much unused capacity in terms of his physical and mental energies, he put his idleness to good use and spent many spare hours on crush fantasies about the wife of the Clerk of Maps. However, he lacked the imagination to sustain a crush on a woman he had never seen. He knew from long experience that the briefest of interactions would be sufficient to feed a decent crush for several months. Once he had seen her corkscrew curls, he would be able to withdraw again, happy to undertake the sweet labour of his crush alone and in secret.

But he was by nature shy with his passions. His confidence had to be imbibed. The greater the passion, the greater his need to consume bottles of confidence.

Using his supposed need to borrow her husband's theodolite as an excuse, the town drunk called to the wife of the Clerk of Maps at a time when he knew her husband would be away at the conference.

When the wife of the Clerk of Maps answered the door, she did indeed have enchanting corkscrew curls, which, to the town drunk, bespoke a quiet wildness.

She said she read the local newspaper and admired his many reported adventures.

As he stood in the hall, he saw that she was drinking red wine. There was melancholy music playing. She said she had been dancing alone and asked the town drunk whether he ever did the same.

Disarmed by her candour, the town drunk's shyness once again overcame him, in response to which he drank quickly the wine she poured for him. He found himself restarting stories midway, repeating jokes he had already told and asking her questions that trailed off. Bewitched by her corkscrew curls, he even declared his crush, breaking the only unbreakable rule of crushes.

Later that evening, the town drunk woke to find himself on the couch, covered by a woman's winter coat. The Clerk of Maps' wife was sitting on a stool in the kitchen, now drinking white wine, and watching over him. There was different melancholy music playing in the background.

The town drunk's head roared with a hangover and his ballooning embarrassment.

He mumbled the meekest of excruciating goodbyes and left with the theodolite.

As town drunk, he had many times acted in a way that was beneath himself, but to suffer such shame before his crush was especially scalding. On the heavy walk home, he resolved to disavow his town drunkenness and his crushes

When he changed for bed that night, to his surprise, he found rose petals in his briefs.

Ghost Mountain

At Ghost Mountain, the first visitors would arrive about an hour before the sun started shining on the mountain it knew nothing about. Human voices, initially audible as chatter and incidental talk – not conversation as such – would quieten on the approach. Seeing the desire line that had recently been cut around the base of the mountain, the people would follow some instinct of conformity and walk it in a clockwise direction. As the sun rose, so too would the temptation to view it from the summit, though it was not an especially high mountain and the top was little nearer the sun than the base was. Still, those who came to see a sunrise, saw a sunrise.

As the day would wear on, more and more people would arrive and walk their way around the base, and over the weeks that followed, more and more of those doing so started coming on a regular basis. There was an ineffability to the experience that spoke to them.

At nighttime Ghost Mountain would stand alone in the bone-white moonlight.

But in time, there were those who, encouraged, step-by-step, to observe the change in the mountain and the change in themselves, would continue walking around Ghost Mountain throughout the night in a slow caravan that replenished itself as new shifts of walkers relieved those who were tiring.

And so it began that there was a perpetual circuit of walkers at Ghost Mountain, for which it became famous all over again.

Driving to Ghost Mountain

It was a warm night and Ruth and Ocho lay awake with the bedclothes folded back. Ruth wore a slip but was still too hot. Ocho wore a vest and was also too hot. They both thought about Hee-Haw and the fact that they had not had it for some time. The thought of Hee-Haw felt like a third presence in the room. Even though they were hot they didn't feel the right sort of heat in the Hee-Haw part of their bodies. Eventually, Ruth said "Good night, Ocho," adding that maybe they could do it in the morning. They had agreed many times that it was better in the morning than nighttime. At night, they were always so tired and their heads full of the day.

But the next morning, when Ocho woke up, Ruth was already downstairs, making breakfast by the sound of it. She was taking a long time. After waiting longer than he could bear, Ocho realised that there would be no morning Hee-Haw. Full of entitlement and bitterness, he decided to discover himself. He would replace Ruth's face in his mind with another face. But it was pointless. He was no good at imagining faces and there was to be no satisfaction for him.

When he came downstairs, Ruth explained that she was making the picnic for their trip to Ghost Mountain with Carthage and Clare. She asked if cooked ham was OK for his sandwich. Ocho loved cooked ham but said otherwise. He said that he had been looking forward to butter and peanut butter sandwiches. Ever since he found out that peanut butter was not made from peanuts and butter, he had started adding butter. It wasn't as nice as ham, but he wanted to be difficult that morning. First, because he felt cheated out of Hee-Haw but also now, secondly, because he thought of Carthage. Whenever he saw Carthage in one place he saw him everywhere. He imagined that Ruth hadn't wanted Hee-Haw because she was thinking of Carthage. That she was making the picnic for them all so that she could do something nice for Carthage. That she had bought the quality cooked ham for Carthage specially. So, Ocho made his own sandwiches from butter and peanut butter. But just like when he tried to discover himself, his attempt at revenge misfired. Ruth didn't even realise she was being punished, and Ocho ended up with an inferior lunch that he would regret all day.

Carthage and Clare called later that morning. They had arranged that Carthage would do the driving, in return for which Ruth had offered to make a picnic. Sitting in the back, behind Carthage, made Ocho feel like he was the child and Carthage was the father. Ruth sat in the back, too, behind Clare. That meant she could speak diagonally to Carthage, who could speak back through the rear-view mirror. Ocho wanted to have a diagonal chat with Clare but didn't know what to say. From the way the light shone through the window he could see that Clare's hair had some red in it. He had always thought it was dark brown. The light also showed up the fine peach hairs on her cheek. As he was staring at them, Clare turned to him. So, it was true, he thought – women *can* tell when they are being looked at. To cover himself, Ocho asked Clare how work was going.

"Usual schmusual.," said Clare.

They stopped at the level crossing for the crosstown train. Carthage asked Ocho how work was going for him. Ocho felt like he was being included only because he couldn't keep up with the conversation. He didn't like talking about his job as he didn't have the proper vocabulary for describing what he did. It always sounded like a job anyone could do.

"I'm thinking of changing, actually," he said.

"Really?" said Ruth.

"Really?" said Carthage.

Everyone except Clare had said "Really?"

"But I probably won't," said Ocho and turned to look out the window at the crosstown train approaching from the right. If they drove through the barrier and the train crashed into Carthage, he thought, Clare would become single and it would be Ruth who would have something to worry about. Or maybe they would all be crushed in the collision.

Carthage turned the radio on – Classic Hits. Clare passed around some boiled sweets she took from the glove box. Two conversation killers in one, thought Ocho.

As they drove on the road out of town, where the countryside began, Ocho stared out at the fields and hedges and thought about how boring it all looked. Where are all the animals, he thought. Why do they build such small houses on such big fields, he wondered.

Ruth and Clare started their own private conversation through the headrest. Ocho hoped that stupid bastard Carthage wouldn't start one on their side. He was overthinking and bit into his boiled sweet without meaning to. The middle was a gooey, medicinal blackcurrant syrup that released pungent vapour into his nostrils. Were they cough sweets? Who keeps cough sweets in their glove box?

"It's up here," said Carthage, slowly turning off the road into a field.

It had taken as long as one car sweet.

"We could have walked," said Ocho. His voice was phlegmy and alien-like from the sweet.

"Looks like they've put a temporary car park in to stop people parking on the road," said Carthage. "Locals probably didn't like it."

They followed a path of flattened grass with traffic cones marking the way. It was like the parking at a music festival. People were walking either side of them and sometimes in front of them too. There were older people in androgynous outdoor clothes. There were people with tattoos – the fashion-able-looking type and the violent-looking type. There were parents carrying children on their bodies. Carthage crawled in first gear.

As the mountain came into view, they went quiet.

"You can see why it's called Ghost Mountain, anyway", said Ocho. "Kind of underwhelming."

Nobody answered. Carthage turned off the radio.

"Wow," said Ruth.

"You can sort of feel it, can't you?" said Carthage. "A charge in the air or something."

Ocho looked to Clare, hoping she would say something sensible.

A man in a hi-vis jacket guided them into a parking spot. Carthage thanked him loudly. You're not his friend, thought Ocho. Carthage pulled in and closed everyone's windows with the driver's master switch, dumping Ocho's elbow from where he was resting it.

As Ocho unpacked the car, Ruth stood and absorbed the image of Ghost Mountain. She was transfixed. Carthage and Clare exchanged some quiet words that Ocho didn't hear.

"Where do you want to have the picnic?" asked Ocho.

Carthage swivelled around.

"We were going to go for a walk first. Around Ghost Mountain – how does that sound?" he said.

"I thought we were having a picnic?" said Ocho.

"We've brought food to keep us going, but it's not a picnic, as such," said Ruth. "We're not twelve!"

They all laughed. All except Ocho, that is.

"How about you, Clare?" asked Ocho.

"Oh, I don't know. I think I'll sit and sketch for a while."

"Sketching?" said Ocho. "I didn't know you could draw?"

She turned to him and took a pause before saying: "It's my job."

Ocho digested this for a few frozen moments. Then said: "Oh."

"Are you coming, or what?" asked Ruth.

"I might chill out here and have a bite to eat. Wait and see if a full-size mountain shows up."

"Ok, so," said Carthage. "If you get bored you know where we are – unless the mountain disappears again!"

Ruth and Carthage went off with enthusiasm into the thin stream of walkers who were approaching Ghost Mountain.

Clare took out a picnic blanket and an oversized sketch pad and sat on a patch of grass away from the car, away from Ocho.

I thought she worked in graphic design or something, Ocho said to himself. I thought that was all about lettering and things.

Ocho sat back in the car and unwrapped his butter and peanut butter sandwiches. The filling had congealed in the middle and it tore at the bread when he tried to separate the slices. It would still taste OK, he thought. He felt a harsh scratch on the slack skin between his thumb and forefinger. Bastard wasp, he said. Bastard Carthage, he thought. He jumped out of the car and tried to wave the wasp away but it flew faster than he could swipe. He threw the sandwich onto the back seat. When the wasp followed it, he slammed all the doors to shut it in.

His heart was thudding. He looked over at Ghost Mountain and thought he could make out Ruth and Carthage walking so closely together that they seemed to be one person. Clare was sitting serenely, a short distance away, sketching. Ocho rubbed the skin between his thumb and forefinger, gazing through the car window at the wasp crawling all over his sandwich.

What that everything was

The overseas landowner was waiting to see his line manager. Nobody said boss anymore.

He had wanted to write to the executrix of his father's estate to ask whether, in so many words, he was rich now, without conveying that he was overly interested in money. It was tiring being broke all the time. He had a job and somewhere to live and he could pay his way in the world, but that was about it. Where would he find the stamina to keep that up for another few decades. It would be nice not to have to worry about all that. He had struggled with formulating the email back to the executrix and had included so many qualifiers and caveats that they hadn't answered his question. She had suggested a meeting, which would mean traveling back to his country and the town where he had grown up. However, he didn't have sufficient savings to pay for the trip. That is, he didn't have sufficient capacity on his credit card. He wondered whether he could ask her to lend him some money in the meantime and then deduct it from the grand total when it came time to settle up. The problem was that any email to that effect made him feel like a bad person.

His line manager invited him into her office just as she was finishing a conference call. She was standing and leaning on the desk. She looked like someone vomiting into a sink. At first he sat down, then he stood up because she was still standing, but then he sat down again.

After she had ended the call he explained that he needed some time off work because his father had died. He chose his words carefully. He didn't say that his father had *just* died. She said she was sorry to hear that. She wanted to know whether it was sudden. He told her, yes, that it was sudden. The suddenness was now part of his story. He made a mental note to remember that. He said he needed time off work to deal with everything, without saying what that everything was. Without saying that he was possibly rich now.

She was understanding and told him that he was entitled to two bereavement days and then whatever annual or unpaid leave he wanted. Things were quiet, she said. She asked whether he had brothers or sisters. He said he had not. She asked about his mother and he explained that she was already dead. His line manager's face made a compound expression that included sympathy and understanding but not sadness or over-involvement as such.

At home, he broke the news to his housemates, who were people he hardly knew. He explained that it was sudden. He didn't mention anything about it being recent. The male housemate said sorry, man. The female housemate gave him a hug. He said he would be away for a few days so he could take care of everything. He didn't say what that everything was. And he didn't say that he had decided to use his portion of this month's rent payment to fund the trip.

Ruth not with you?

Ocho had gone for a run for the first time in months. He was trying to reconnect with his body but his body wasn't ready to reconnect. His lungs got tired before his turnaround point. The walk back felt a lot longer than the run out had been.

Ruth was still out when he returned, though he didn't know where. They weren't the sort of couple who texted each other with their movements. He liked that about her and she liked that about him. None of this "I'm leaving now" or "I'm on the train" or "There's fish defrosted in the fridge." They laughed at couples who did that. They liked joking in bed making up stupid things that those sorts of couples said. Lately, when Ocho made those jokes he thought of Carthage and Clare as the couple he had in mind.

Ocho walked around eating a bowl of jelly and waiting for his body to stop sweating so he could shower. He liked that jelly was a drink you could eat. He read a text from his mother saying that his father was sick. A bit of a bug, she said. Ocho texted back to say he would call over. Did they need any chicken? No, his mother texted back. They hadn't even started the chicken he brought last time. What Ocho really meant was whether they would make him dinner or did he have to cook dinner at home before going there. Older people are so literal, he thought.

Ocho brought over some fruitcake he had found in the cupboard. Ruth must have bought it.

He thought his mother looked tired when she answered the door. He told her so.

"I was up and down all night. Your father had the runs," she said.

"Runs aren't so bad," said Ocho.

"Ruth not with you?"

His mother gave him a bowl of chicken soup. She had made a batch of it for his father during the night. Ocho's mother was amazing at looking after people when they were sick. Ocho, on the other hand, usually defaulted to thinking "It's probably nothing" whenever he heard someone was sick. It was because he made so much of his own troubles and didn't like to expend energy on other people's troubles unless he was sure they were worse than his. His mother was different. She emptied herself into other people's troubles.

He pushed the bedroom door open gently. His father's eyes were closed but he said to come in. Ocho announced himself and his father's face brightened a little.

Ocho sat on the bed with his bowl of chicken soup. His father misunderstood and took the bowl from Ocho and started slurping it. Ocho fixed the pillow into position to support his father's back.

"This is good chicken," said his father.

"I got it at the butcher's," said Ocho.

"This is different chicken. The one you brought is still in the freezer. Your mother wasn't sure whether yours was battery or free range – do you know?"

"I dunno, butchered chicken," said Ocho. "Dead chicken. Who cares if it had a nice life?"

They sat together quietly as Ocho watched his father eat. Ocho felt hungry. After all, jelly is more of a drink.

"Ruth not with you?" his father asked.

"She's out somewhere."

"'Somewhere? Don't you know where your wife is?"

"People aren't like that these days, checking up on each other."

Ocho had forgotten how boring sickness was. He sat, perched on the bed, and looked around. His parents had nothing of note in their bedroom. It could have been anyone's bedroom. They had no photos of him.

"Have you been to the new mountain yet?" his father asked.

"We went once. Full of wasps," said Ocho.

"I heard people were doing pilgrimages around it – is it a religious thing?"

"Mostly day trippers and nutcases I think. And the Satanists, I guess. I wouldn't bother if I were you. But bring plenty of insect cream if you do."

"Hmmm. Maybe when I'm better."

"I heard it's the runs. That's not so bad."

Ocho took his father's empty bowl and helped him settle back to bed.

"Rest is best," said his father, repeating one of Ocho's mother's catchphrases.

Ocho looked in on his mother before he left. She had dozed off and her head was tilted back with her mouth open. Ocho saw that she was missing more teeth than he would have guessed. He didn't want to kiss her forehead in case he woke her.

When Ocho returned home, Ruth was still out. He made some more jelly to let it set overnight for the next day. His back was stiff from sitting on his father's bed. His legs were stiff from his run.

He opened the cupboard to look for food but all he saw were ingredients.

Half Day

Ruth had taken the afternoon off work to go back to Ghost Mountain. On her first visit, it had been the picnic and she was walking with Carthage. He had kept talking the whole time. He spoke about how interested he was in coming to walk on Ghost Mountain. He said he had seen it from the road and driven as far as the car park but this was his first time on the mountain proper. As they walked around it, he narrated his experience. No thought went unexpressed. She realised that Carthage was a younger soul than she had thought.

Ruth's second visit felt like her first true visit. She walked clockwise on the path that now scarred the base of Ghost Mountain. There was a handful of other walkers. They were quiet, dedicated types. No day-trippers. Nobody walking anti-clockwise. Nobody walking up to the summit.

At first, Ruth's mind was chatty, like Carthage's mind had been. There was newness, strangeness and a little exhilaration. She thought about whether clockwise walking was bad for her legs and whether it was harder on her right leg or her left leg. She thought about whether she should have told Ocho she was coming. She thought about whether she should have told Carthage she was coming. She thought about the dog who choked on Ghost Mountain. But her imagination soon stopped roiling.

Ghost Mountain impressed her.

The feeling of Ghost Mountain impressed her.

The idea of Ghost Mountain impressed her.

She could see herself clearly on Ghost Mountain. Ordinarily, her mind was like a zorbing ball and it felt like she was trapped and bouncing around inside it. But on Ghost Mountain, she felt like her mind had no boundary.

This impressed her also.

But what impressed her most was the way Ghost Mountain had appeared. Not that it had appeared suddenly. Not that it had appeared mysteriously. What impressed her most was that it had appeared and had no message.

Glass the size of an engagement ring diamond

The woman whose dog had choked sat alone in her house eating sausages she had bought at the butcher's, a shop she visited less often since her dog died. She cut her sausages like she always did, lengthways down the middle. A sausage is the same width as the gullet. She knew – had always known – that they are a choking hazard.

"It's not like I didn't think of these things," she said to herself.

It seemed like any time she had something tough to swallow, she thought of her dog.

The dog's absence was all around the house. The dog was omniabsent. She had tried to escape the absence but it followed her everywhere. She had various metaphors she used to describe the feeling, but nothing could shift what today she called the heavy stone of loneliness in her stomach.

A brick crashed through her living room window and landed on her couch, leaving pieces of glass the size of engagement ring diamonds all over the upholstery. She was feeling so sad, she hardly got a fright.

Attached to the brick – an inferior type of brick to the ones she was used to – was a message. It said: "How come you know about theodolites?"

She looked through the window and saw the town drunk walking slowly out of her driveway. He wore crumpled chinos.

She called out her front door after him. He turned around slowly and stood facing her.

"I can pay for the window," he said. "In small amounts over a long period of time."

"Why did you ask me about theodolites?"

"It has been on my mind," he said.

"Well, it's personal and I don't want to get into it," she said.

"I understand. I apologise for troubling you in your grief. Losing a dog is the hardest thing."

"It's not the worst thing," she said, "but it is hard. Would you like to come in?"

"No thank you," he replied.

"But I need you to clean up the glass," she said.

The town drunk did as she asked. He cut his hand reaching down the back of the cushions to find any shards he had missed.

"I suppose I deserve that," he said.

She found him a plaster while he washed the cut.

"My family are all engineers. They all have theodolites," she said. "So that's why."

"I see," he said.

"But we're estranged, so I don't see their theodolites anymore."

The town drunk thought about this.

"Would you go to their funerals?" he asked.

"If they all died at once, then yes. If they died individually, then probably not," she answered.

"I too am estranged from my family," he said.

"Is that because you're an alcoholic?"

"I am a drunk, not an alcoholic. And anyway, I've decided to stop all that. I'm estranged because sometimes you need to break up with people. The basic rules of relationships also apply to families."

"What happened?"

"We fell out of love."

"Do you miss them?"

The town drunk thought for a minute.

"Before I broke up with my family, I often doubted myself. I no longer do that."

She put the plaster on his hand. He had cut the fleshy part of the palm. Plasters were mainly designed for fingers, so it didn't fit as well as she would have liked.

"You get some things right, at least," she said.

"Like what?"

She handed him his coat.

"Thanks for not asking me if I'm going to get another dog," she said.

He looked at her squarely.

"How could anyone think to ask such a thing," he said.

Homecoming

The overseas landowner met with the executrix of his father's estate to find out whether, in a manner of speaking, he was rich now.

He was asset-rich, the executrix said.

He didn't understand what that hyphenated form of richness meant.

The executrix explained that he had inherited land, but not money. But the land was worth money. However, you couldn't spend land. You had to convert land into money in order to spend it. She showed him a map. It was like his father had bought all the black squares on a chess board but none of the white squares. The overseas landowner didn't understand chess so he was not sure, by analogy, which type of piece (if any) could only move on black squares. In any event, he had sworn off metaphors. These black squares were his father's life's work. He had been estranged from his father, so he was unsure how to interpret the bequest. He asked the executrix whether the bequest was an olive branch.

The will did not mention his father's intentions, she said, and it contained no metaphors. What would you like to do, she asked him. Did he want to buy up any adjoining plots? Did he want to sell any land? Did he want the land valued? Did he want to make enquiries? What did he want to do about the new mountain on his land and the people walking around it in contravention of the Court order?

They all sounded like good questions. Great questions.

The landowner said he wanted a house and that he didn't want to have to work anymore. Could that be arranged?

The executrix said there were houses on the land. His father had lived in the cottage on the plot where the new mountain was. There was another house that was rented out on a different plot. He had tenants now.

This was new information. He was not only a landowner but a landlord. The term 'lord' in the word implied status.

The executrix drove him out to see the land. Sometimes she pointed at fields from the car without stopping, and other times she parked and stepped out to explain something about rights that were his or weren't his.

They stopped outside a house that had a family living in it. The family's father was in the garden. The executrix explained details about the house as if the father wasn't there. The overseas landowner made eye contact with the father and called out a nervous, unreturned greeting.

How could I be his landlord, he thought. He has a car and a family and money to pay for all the things in the house. I don't have any money. I only have land.

He then understood that land was worth more than money. If you sold land you got money, but if you held land you had both the money value of the land and the power value of the land. That made him sick in his stomach.

Lastly, they drove to the house his father had bought and lived in after their estrangement. It was an ugly bunker of a building and had several barns and sheds and stores around it. The buildings were huddled together as if for warmth, despite being on a large plot of land. The house faced a mountain that people were walking around. The executrix told the astonishing story of how the mountain had appeared and how the people were walking in contravention of a Court order his father had secured.

Inside, his father's house was old fashioned and basic. In the living room there was a heater beside the largest chair. His father owned so much property and yet, by the end, took up so little space, he thought.

The executrix suggested that the landowner should sleep on things. It was a lot to take in.

That night, the landowner ate a hotel dinner that he paid for with this month's rent.

Stir Fry

Ruth spent most of her time at Ghost Mountain these days. Ocho presumed she was with stupid bastard Carthage but took comfort that at least she slept at home each night. That was the main thing. If ever she started sleeping at Ghost Mountain he would never get her back. He didn't complain to her about being out so much, especially as doing so would invite her to explain why, which he sensed would not be good for him. Just in case, he had prepared some comeback lines on the subject. "Well, at least I'm not up a mountain half the time." Or "don't blame me – I'm always here if you want me, but I can't stop you going out." He wasn't interested in winning arguments but he didn't like losing them either.

They were having a lot less Hee-Haw than usual, but some was better than none. It was pure maintenance Hee-Haw. Enough to burn off the body's excess energy but nothing too intimate and they went straight to sleep afterwards.

Ocho was still breaking-in his boots. They hurt so much that he hardly left the house and when in the house he limited his movements to save his poor feet. He would wear his slippers for a while, but wanted to be wearing his boots in case Ruth came in. He thought she might say "How are the boots?" or "How are your feet doing?" and this would make her care about him.

They had always split the house chores between them in that he did his jobs and she did her jobs. He had considered it fair as they each had agreed to do specific tasks and so long as they stuck to that, what was the problem? He knew his list was lighter than hers but he reasoned that she had chosen her jobs because she liked them done her way. He had wanted them to get a cleaner, to save Ruth work, he said. She said it would be ridiculous given that they had spare time but no spare money. But since Ruth had started going to Ghost Mountain she had stopped doing her jobs. Ocho didn't know whether she was on strike or resentful, or simply more interested in something else now. The floors were looking dirtier these days especially since his boots dragged mud into the house.

Ruth's absence left Ocho to do his own cooking all the time. They used to take turns. When Ruth cooked she tended to make something from a cookbook. When Ocho made dinner he usually made stir fry. He liked stir fry. All it involved was some chopping and then throwing everything in together. He used chicken and bought it already diced to avoid the hassle of cutting it and the germs and everything. Ruth asked him if he ever felt bad about eating so much chicken. He decided to think about it a bit more over the days that followed. He wasn't reflecting on his chicken habits per se – he wasn't the type to take on the world's problems – but he wanted to have a better answer if it came up again. He decided he would answer by asking what would happen to the chickens if we stopped eating them. Farmers don't want pets. The farmers would kill the chickens anyway to use their farms for something people wanted to buy. Chickens would be wiped out. Would they thank us for that? He ran through these lines every now and again so that he could deliver them the right way. Like how stupid bastard Carthage would deliver them. Whatever you could say about Carthage, he was certainly good at delivering smug remarks.

Ocho could see that whenever he was alone for too long he got bored and that when he got bored the rat's brain in his gut took over. Whenever the boredom and his rat's brain became too much, he would visit his parents for a break. But he wasn't that bored yet.

Ruth

It was true that Ruth was spending more and more time at Ghost Mountain. After all, she thought, it was her time to spend.

She could think of it as exercise time. She could think of it as alone-time. She could think of it as free time. She could think of it as spare time. But for whose sake did she need to categorise it? Who was she accountable to? She had become emboldened about confronting her own self-justifications. The more she walked clockwise around Ghost Mountain the clearer she got, and the clearer she saw things.

Carthage had joined her this time. He talked the whole way round. She had come almost every day since that first time, but this was only his second visit. He had never walked around Ghost Mountain alone. He had only come when Ruth was there. Ruth read into this. Ruth was not stupid. She knew about plausible deniability. She knew that a person could find many good reasons for doing something when they wanted to do it for a bad reason.

She sometimes thought she should sleep with Carthage to cure him and get rid of him. She was not attracted to Carthage. He was not unattractive, but she wasn't interested in him aesthetically. Whenever he opened his mouth, she wanted to stuff straw into it. Why couldn't he simply walk around Ghost Mountain? Why did he give so much feedback? Was it because he wanted feedback? At least Ocho never wanted feedback. She wondered whether she had ever thought of Ocho aesthetically. Her body was attracted to him when they were in bed. His was warm and firm, whereas hers was warm and soft. But when Ocho was clothed, her eyes didn't react to him. It was a tactile attraction not visual. In that sense it felt impersonal.

Carthage said he had been reading about mountains. Ruth thought she would have to either sleep with him or stuff straw into his mouth. She wouldn't sleep with him though. She could not do that to Clare. She didn't know Clare well and suspected that nobody knew Clare well. But she could see that Clare was the type of person who got underestimated all the time. She thought that Carthage underestimated Clare. She also thought that Carthage underappreciated Clare. She thought that he underestimated her because he underappreciated her. Ruth was not interested in hurting Clare. Ruth was not interested in hurting Ocho. The temptation to stuff straw into Carthage's mouth was not a sign that she wanted to hurt him either. It would have been her way of waking him up.

"Sorry, I seem to be talking a lot," he said, exhaling a brief laughing noise.

"Let's be quiet for a while," she said.

When the sun started going down, Carthage offered her a lift home.

"I'm going to spend the night here," she said.

She felt that if Carthage tried to say anything she would stuff straw into his mouth. She wanted to be ready. She wanted her timing to be immaculate.

His lips opened, but Ruth spoke a half-beat before him. "Tell Clare that if she ever wants to come to Ghost Mountain or stay overnight here, tell her that her friend, Ruth, would like that."

"Sure, sure, sure," said Carthage.

Ruth walked late into the night and slept outside in a sleeping bag among a group of other people in sleeping bags.

She thought they were sleeping but then one of them asked her, "What are you laughing at?"

Ruth had been laughing at the idea of Carthage driving home with his mouth full of straw.

The Tenant

The overseas landowner, who was now simply a landowner, had been reflecting on his new position. Or positions, plural. He had recently become an orphan, a landowner and a landlord. Of these three it was the last that weighed on him most heavily. As someone who had practically exhausted his savings – that is, he had nearly reached the limit on his credit card – his sympathies lay naturally with those who worked hard but whom the world abused. While he was not political as such, his inner compass was, he believed, aligned to common sense and fairness. He could not enjoy his wealth at others' expense.

His indecision over his father's estate was largely due to his uncertainty about his tenant. If he held on to the land, he would have power over another man and his family. But if he sold it, the land would surely be bought by a less enlightened soul, who might evict or otherwise mistreat the tenant. He knew nothing of the tenant but fancied that he was a man who had known his father and who was bound to the land in a way that he, the landowner, was not. The landowner had rights of property and law, but the tenant may well have held superior rights of affinity. It was a flaw in the workings of the world that the former counted for everything and the latter for nothing at all. He had seriously considered assigning the cottage to the man but thought better of it. Grand gestures bespeak condescension, he thought to himself, and then wrote the phrase down so that he might use it again.

He had a contemplative breakfast at his hotel. Breakfast was included in the price, and so was the only meal he was able to enjoy without anxiety. On a full stomach, and while soaking up his spilled egg yolk with some toast, he decided to visit his tenant and speak to him candidly. He thought he would wait until mid-morning, reasoning – considerately – that the tenant might be having breakfast with his own family.

On the walk over there, he thought about how he and the tenant might become warmer acquaintances and perhaps friends. The tenant could become a source of insight into his father. The tenant may have all sorts of practical advice about the land and its management. Perhaps the tenant would even become his estate manager in lieu of rent.

The landowner looked out for some blackthorn that he might use as a walking stick on his way.

He was glad to see the tenant in the garden when he arrived. The tenant was weeding, which he thought was a good omen.

He explained who he was.

He explained who his father was.

He explained in a long-winded way his view of things, which also included his views on the world in general. He explained about grand gestures and condescension.

The tenant told him that if he fucked him around he would break his jaw.

The landowner reflected on this as he walked back to the hotel.

Theodolite Blues

The town drunk received a bizarre series of rambling drunken late-night voice messages from the Clerk of Maps. There was something about the conference and a girl and his wife and a lift, and some line about hoping Ghost Mountain had not disappeared or he'd have nothing to talk about at next year's conference. In his final message he had observed sadly that Ghost Mountain had stayed while his wife had disappeared.

The town drunk decided he had better check up on him and also return his theodolite.

He found the Clerk of Maps unshaven and sitting on the front doorstep. His face was red and puffy and he was holding a bottle of brandy.

"I have your theodolite. Sorry I've had it so long."

"Keep it," said the Clerk of Maps quietly. His posture was slack.

"What's with the brandy?"

"Here – have some."

The town drunk declined and explained that he had disavowed drinking, without saying why. "It's not like you to be drunk on the step. How did your presentation at the conference go?"

The Clerk of Maps filled the town drunk in on what had happened. His young female colleague had resigned. HQ said she was last seen going up in the lift with the Clerk of Maps at the conference – the rumour mill had done the rest. The Clerk of Maps remarked that the rumour mill was the most efficient industry in the town.

Hesitantly, and in spite of himself, the town drunk asked about the wife of the Clerk of Maps.

The Clerk of Maps confided that his wife had been cool towards him ever since his return from the conference and that they no longer enjoyed their special lunchtimes. These things he had attributed to her jealousy of his newfound renown.

But that morning, as they sat in the waiting room for one of their many appointments with the doctor, she had said she no longer wanted a baby from him. She was leaving him and hoped he understood.

He had said he didn't understand but she left him anyway. She was now staying who-knows-where – he gestured his hands to indicate somewhere vague and far away.

"I've done nothing wrong," he said, despairing. "Nothing."

The Clerk of Maps betrayed no knowledge of the crush or the town drunk's embarrassing social call.

"What would you do in my situation?" he asked. "You're used to finding yourself in a mess, aren't you?"

"You say you did nothing wrong," said the town drunk.

"That's right. Nothing."

"Were your intentions honest?"

"How do you mean?"

"What were you thinking the whole time?"

"I don't know. I was enjoying myself – what's wrong with that?"

He took a swig from the bottle. The town drunk could tell he wasn't used to drinking. Brandy is a sipping drink. The Clerk of Maps winced.

"Seriously," said the Clerk of Maps, "keep the theodolite. I'm not going back to do any more work on that stupid mountain. It was a bad idea ever coming out here. This place is a backwater – no offence." He burped and swallowed back a bit of sick.

The town drunk was halfway home with the theodolite when he thought about the woman whose dog had choked. She still had a broken window.

"Come in," said the woman. "I wasn't expecting to see you again so soon."

"I have inherited this theodolite. I thought you might like it."

"But I don't know how to use it."

"You could learn. It's in your background."

The town drunk stood the tripod in her hallway. He could see that she was impressed once it was set up. Anything that stood by itself seemed to earn its place in the world.

"Will you stay for lunch?" she asked.

"What are you having?"

"Smoked salmon. I can't face the butchers since my dog died. I'm eating more fish now."

The town drunk accepted, though he wasn't a fan of smoked salmon on account of the texture.

She served lunch with lots of bits and pieces – dips and breads and salads. He wasn't used to that. Too much cleaning up afterwards.

"What do you work at?" she asked him.

"I'm self-employed."

"What do you employ yourself to do?"

"Whatever I like."

She put a dollop of some white sauce on her smoked salmon. He ate his neat. No bread or anything.

"What do you do?" he asked.

"I took early retirement. I was a teacher."

"What did you teach – engineering?"

"My brothers were engineers. We're estranged anyway. I taught art – portraiture mainly."

"Do you still paint?"

"I was never that good. Anyway, I don't have anyone to paint and I'm not worth painting myself."

The town drunk knew to shut up rather than saying anything about how she looked

The smoked salmon had that snakeskin feel to it. He didn't like the texture in his mouth. He swallowed before he had chewed it fully and it unravelled in his throat. He couldn't breathe. He couldn't cough it up. He knew that if you were coughing you weren't choking. Whereas he was silently choking.

The woman poured herself a cup of tea. She looked up to offer him some and saw him sitting rigidly, gripping his cutlery. She jumped up and tried to Heimlich the problem away but she couldn't get enough purchase. She started slapping him hard on his shoulders, swinging her arm all the way back like a tennis shot. The room was quiet otherwise.

The town drunk started coughing. She reached her fingers into his mouth to pull out a long, congealed rope of half-chewed smoked salmon. She wrapped it in a napkin and set it on his side plate.

The woman sat down again. They were both exhausted by the experience.

A long time passed.

"Were you thinking about your dog?" the town drunk asked.

She started to cry quietly.

"I was too," he said.

They spent the rest of the day together keeping each other company. The town drunk fixed her window by putting a sheet of plywood over it.

When it got dark he said that he should be going home.

She thanked him for the theodolite.

He thanked her for stopping him choking.

When it came to the bit where she was supposed to say "Goodnight" she said "Stay" instead.

He put his coat back on the coatrack. He didn't believe in pretending not to want something that he actually wanted. He was finished with crushes but he still had his romantic nature.

She made a bed for him on the floor beside her own bed.

"Good night," she said.

"Sleep well," he said.

They both lay awake. The trees outside the bedroom window made the wind seem noisier than it was.

"You can come in beside me, if you like," she said, softly.

"Are you sure?"

He climbed under her covers and she moved over. He lay in the warmth she had left for him.

"My name is Elaine," she said.

"My name is Dominic," he replied.

They lay facing each other on separate pillows.

"Good night, Dominic."

"Good night, Elaine."

Ok-ishly Decently Fine

Ocho was so sick of stir fry. The vegetables kept coming out slimy. When he ate his chicken, all he could think of was how unlike the animal it looked. And that chickens eat worms. Eating alone was so different to eating with someone else, to eating with Ruth. With Ruth there, he would have been looking at her, and talking as he ate. Eating alone, he looked at his plate and saw it as the indistinguishable mess it was. All browns and greens. With nobody to talk to, he started noticing how unrewarding chewing was. It took so much repetitive effort. Round and round like a washing machine. His cheeks were still full of mush ages after he had swallowed the flavour.

He went to the butcher's to get some fresh inspiration for dinner. Maybe he would buy that meat he had in a restaurant with Ruth once. It was game, she had said. Was it Guinea Fowl? Is that game?

There was a queue in the butcher's, as always. He didn't mind as it proved what a good butcher he was. It was because it was so clean. Clean as a hospital.

A couple of places in front of him he could see Carthage and Clare. Carthage was easy to spot as he was the tallest person in the shop. There was a radio playing behind the counter, so Ocho had to strain to overhear them. They were holding hands and Clare's head rested against Carthage's shoulder.

"So, how was it anyway?" he heard Carthage ask.

"Oh, fine," she said distractedly.

"Fine in a good way or a bad way?"

"Sort of OK-ishly, decently fine," she said and then laughed.

He nudged her playfully and they kissed.

Ocho didn't like the idea of mixing tongues in a butcher's. He tried his best to spy on them without being seen. The butcher gave them a ticket with his bloody hands and they went up to the front of the shop to pay.

When it was Ocho's turn he told the butcher he was bored with his usual dinner and asked him if he sold game. He was still watching Carthage and Clare at the till and mentioned that he had enjoyed Guinea Fowl in a restaurant, so something like that. The butcher said he could sell him some rabbit, but there might be pieces of shot in it, so to mind his teeth. This made Ocho think of where the name "game" came from. It meant food killed for fun. He decided to buy a spiced sausage and some mince instead. He knew how to make spaghetti.

Carthage and Clare were outside. Their meat was double bagged and they had bought a lot of it.

"We thought we saw you in there," said Carthage. He stood too close to Ocho, making him feel small.

"I was buying dinner," he said. He held up his own much lighter bag.

"How have you both been?" asked Carthage.

Clare was smoking. Ocho didn't know she smoked.

"Fine, I suppose," said Ocho. He didn't say OK-ishly, decently fine. "Ruth has been spending a lot of time at Ghost Mountain, but I suppose you knew that already."

Ocho looked at Carthage.

"We haven't been back much, to be honest. I went one other time when it was quiet – saw Ruth there, in fact," said Carthage, "but the whole thing seemed such a hoax, so we haven't returned."

This was news to Ocho. Then who was Ruth with?

"What about your sketches?" Ocho asked Clare.

Clare exhaled her smoke. "Oh, they came out like stupid Pac Man ghosts. I binned them."

Carthage and Clare both laughed. They were holding hands again. Ocho didn't laugh.

That night he lay in bed after his spaghetti. He had made too much pasta so had to keep some for the next day. Why was it so impossible to cook for one person?

He was uneasy in bed. He never liked sleeping alone, ever since he was little. The house noises all sounded like burglars breaking in. What is there to steal, though, he thought. All I have is a laptop and a mobile phone and a tangle of chargers.

He listened for a while. He wondered where Ruth was sleeping. And who she was sleeping with.

Maybe I'll go see my parents tomorrow, he thought. Maybe I'll sleep over.

Night on Ghost Mountain

Ruth was still spending her nights in a sleeping bag at the foot of Ghost Mountain among a small group of regular walkers. She noticed how seldom she thought of Ocho. But she didn't judge herself for that. She didn't judge him either.

Ruth wasn't interested in the other walkers at Ghost Mountain. She wasn't looking to become part of a movement. Ruth didn't feel any affinity with them. Ruth's affinity was with Ghost Mountain. Walking around, she would hear fragments of the other walkers' conversations. Their words travelled round and round with them. Some of the walkers were so full of loneliness. She could hear how the loneliness displaced everything inside them. They were trying to fill themselves with Ghost Mountain.

At night, the walkers would congregate in their sleeping bags. They would eat tinned food and talk away the darkness. Ruth had heard all their theories about Ghost Mountain. Ruth no longer needed her own theories. Her theories had brought her there but now she no longer needed them. Ruth made herself as invisible as possible. She was not one of the walkers who disclosed their personal histories. She was not one of those who couldn't resist organising things. Ruth distrusted organised people. Organised people liked to take over, while pretending they were not taking over. Organised people liked to shape things their way and call it helping. They organised the things outside themselves, but not inside themselves. Some of the walkers proposed lighting a fire to keep away midges. Others suggested that they devise a common shopping list for supplies to avoid doubling-up. One mentioned that it was fine sleeping outside in sleeping bags for now, but it wouldn't be practical once the weather changed and so they needed to plan ahead.

Here we go again, thought Ruth.

A man with dirty nails had made some soup from things he had picked on Ghost Mountain. Everyone was drinking it. Ruth accepted a tin mug of the grey-brown steaming broth. It was like the soup a child would make from grass and stones and puddle water. It was disgusting. It wasn't salty or creamy. The thought reminded her of Ocho, but the memory had no traction.

Ruth sat and drank her awful soup, surrounded by those strange, organised people. She tuned out of their conversations and looked upon the silhouette of Ghost Mountain.

Ghost Mountain had no affinities.

Ghost Mountain was not organised.

Ghost Mountain was Ghost Mountain.

Rotten Bananas

The landowner had left his hotel and moved into his father's old house. He needed to economise as the hotel had consumed almost all his savings, that is, the unused capacity on his credit card and what was left of his monthly rent payment. His father's house was not at all what he might have expected. The only clue that it had been his father's was the pervading smell of a life in decay, much like rotten bananas.

The executrix had been pressing the landowner for a decision. She said that the chequerboard of unconnected land parcels could be sold to the adjoining landowners for agricultural value. In other words, not much. However, there would be a lot of interest in the house that was currently rented out and the plot where his father had lived, which included the huddled buildings, the unenforced Court order and, of course, the new mountain.

The landowner fantasised that if he made a lot of money on the sale of his land – he now referred to it effortlessly as his – then he could do something noble with the rented property. Something that would impress people with its goodness. A gesture that would make people feel in awe of him. If property represented both power and money, then he would take the opportunity to show the better side of power. Against that, if selling the rented property meant he wouldn't have to work ever again, he might have to wait and do something noble later on instead. The decision was also complicated by his fear of his tenant.

The decision about his father's house and the surrounding land, including Ghost Mountain, was more difficult. While he had sworn off using metaphors, he could see how this decision was bound up with his unexamined feelings about his father. As he walked from room to room he found himself putting on his father's voice and commenting. He would stoop going through doorways, as his father would have done, though he was not a tall man. He made silly jokes to himself by saying "Where's the rotten bananas? Who hid the rotten bananas?" in a parody of his father at his worst moments.

He was minding his money and so took a trip into town to pick up some meat for dinner instead of eating out. He asked the butcher for enough meat for seven dinners, to last him the week. The butcher asked if he had a freezer, but the landowner said he didn't know. He asked him how he planned to cook the meat, but the landowner said he didn't know whether his oven was working. He then told the butcher who he was and that he had moved into his father's old house and was still getting used to things. The landowner hadn't intended disclosing so much unbidden, but he felt the pull of unanswered questions in the conversation. The butcher suggested stir fry and weighed up a week's worth of chicken and handed him a ticket with blood on it.

It was only as he was paying at the front of the shop that the landowner decided to invite his tenant over for dinner. It would be nobler to discuss his plans with the man who was most affected. He would surely not break his jaw while they were enjoying a stir fry. And anyway, it was only fair, considering that the landowner was paying for the meat out of his tenant's rent deposit.

Ping Pong

The situation with Ruth had been difficult for Ocho. So long as he had thought of her in terms of stupid bastard Carthage it had made him sad and angry but not confused. Now that Carthage was no longer part of the picture, he was left with a shapeless, nameless enemy spreading through the rat's brain in his gut. It affected his concentration and his sleep and drained his defences, whatever they might be.

After he had finished another flavourless stir fry, he pushed the table against the wall and played ping pong against himself. The rhythm of the shots played a waltz-time of tick-tock-tick, bat-wall-table, calming him. He played while standing in the boots he was still breaking in. But whenever he reached for a shot, they pinched as if to say "Bad shot, you stupid boy!" His unease would then build until he would smash a shot against the wall only to cower from the rebound.

Ocho did not believe in analysing things. He only wanted Ruth to come home. It wasn't just about Hee-Haw or having company. They had grown together. He was like one of those climbing plants he could visualise but couldn't remember the name of, and she was the trellis. What she got out of it all, he couldn't say.

He drove to Ghost Mountain to see her or at least to watch her. His feet hurt the whole way. Whenever he hit the brakes or the clutch his boots pinched. It was painful but in a way it was a relief to have a pain he could understand.

Ghost Mountain looked subdued in the grey light. There was a group of a dozen or so walkers doing circuits around the scar at its base. The walkers were mostly wearing rain gear and it was hard to tell which were the men and which were the women. He stood for a minute on a grassy mound and trained his eyes until he could see Ruth in among them. He decided to wait at the foot of the mountain and meet Ruth when she came around the turn, as if she were his suitcase at a baggage carousel.

She waved and smiled when she saw him but didn't stop. Ocho waited until she came around a second time and then climbed up to the path and jogged a little to catch up with her. His boots hurt.

"Could we stop for a minute?" Ocho asked.

Ruth stepped out of the group and let the others pass between them.

"Everything OK?" she asked when they were alone.

"I don't know. I suppose I wanted to check that with you."

"What's on your mind?"

"Well, are you up here taking some time out, or are you trying to get away from me? Are we still married or are you sleeping with Carthage or somebody else?"

"It's none of those things."

Ocho didn't know whether this meant they were still married.

"Am I supposed to reason with you or negotiate or argue or what?" he asked.

"None of those sound like a good idea," said Ruth.

Her face was like a mirror to him. He couldn't see into it. It was shining but not at him, nor because of him. It felt like his own anxieties, whatever they were, were bouncing back.

"Would you prefer to get back to your walking?" he asked.

"I think so."

"Without me?"

"None of this is about you, OK? Good or bad."

Ruth dipped her head to retrieve eye contact with Ocho, whose head hung low.

"Here they come again," he said. "They certainly keep going."

Ocho leaned in for a small kiss on her cheek, but her boots made her taller than usual so it landed on her chin. She kissed him on his cheek and said "Bye."

She fell into step with the group and shed his company like a dress she was stepping out of.

Portrait

Elaine, whose dog had choked on Ghost Mountain, was painting Dominic, the town drunk. He sat on a stool wearing jeans and had his top off for some reason. He had a pigeon chest.

"I'm nearly finished, but I'm warning you, I'm a little out of practice," she said. "Look that way a bit. And close your mouth – teeth are hard to do."

"I don't mind if it's not flattering, so long as it's a good likeness"

"Likeness isn't that important," she said. "Nobody knows if the real Mona Lisa looked like the painting."

Dominic tried to hold a concentrated pose but he was soon daydreaming. His leg felt numb and he became bored. He thought about what boredom was. It was just thinking about time. He liked looking at Elaine working. She winked one eye and then the other, trying to see him clearly. She was staring at him yet he felt invisible.

"OK, it's done," she said.

He put his shirt on and walked around the easel to look at the painting.

"It's beautiful," he said.

"The eyes are off," Elaine said. "I rushed them."

"You captured my posture all the same. It's definitely me. And I like how you put a happy child and a dog playing on the mountain in the background."

"The whole thing is so stupid," said Elaine.

"Please don't say that."

He noticed Elaine was tearful.

"Hey, what's the matter? Why are you crying?"

She put down her brushes and dabbed her eye with the corner of her apron.

"It's ok, I'm fine," she said, collecting herself. She straightened up. "I think I'm pregnant. In fact, I am pregnant."

Dominic rubbed his belly under his shirt.

"But, but … how? Aren't you about my age – can women still have babies in their fifties?"

"What a pointless question."

"Sorry. I suppose I hadn't considered the possibility."

She dropped her brush into the jar of water with a clink and a quiet splash.

"Is it … is it mine?" he asked. "Not that I'm suggesting …"

"Yes, it's yours," she said, her voice quivering. She addressed his portrait rather than looking at him directly. "It was my first time."

He took her hand.

"Everything is going to be ok," he said. "We'll do this together."

She released his hand

"I never thought I'd have a child with the town drunk, that's all. I'm sorry, but that's how people will look at it. I never saw myself that way. I'm ashamed. It's humiliating."

A brick crashed through the window. It had a note attached. Dominic untied the note and read it.

"It says: *I want my theodolite back*," he read.

They looked through the broken window and saw the former Clerk of Maps walking back down the driveway, holding a bottle of brandy by the neck.

"Looks like we have a new town drunk," he said, putting his arm around Elaine.

She leaned in and rested her head against his pigeon chest.

Bitter Soup

Ruth found herself falling deeper and deeper into Ghost Mountain.

The time she spent there seemed like time suspended. She felt like she was both inside and outside her body. Ruth carried this sensation with her like a secret. It excited and energised her. She wondered if others could tell. If they could see it in her. She felt like light. She felt like slowed-down light. The particles in her body felt like they were mixing freely with the particles around her.

That evening, the walkers waited for the sun to go down. They had organised a celebration or commemoration or festival. The organised people always seemed to be carried away with something or other. They had a whole story about why the date was significant. It all sounded simplistic to Ruth. They were building a bonfire and playing crude, repetitive music. Drugs were involved. Some more soup had been made from the herbs found on Ghost Mountain. Ruth was handed a bowl of it and drank it back. It scalded her tongue. The aftertaste was bitter.

She zoned out. She enjoyed her separateness and yet she felt interchangeable with everything around her. Perhaps she was lucid dreaming. Dreaming but awake in her dreams. She felt light but constricted. There was a tightness in her. Her eyes flickered. Her tongue felt huge in her mouth. She tried to speak but her tongue was spongy and lethargic. It filled her throat. There was too little space for air to pass through. She was listless and drunk from a lack of oxygen. Her eyesight was vague and her thoughts seemed to lag behind what she saw. People were lying around, but not sleeping. No talking or shouting. A few involuntary noises. Groans and heaves and such.

Everything was shutting down. Ruth couldn't move her body. There was a frisson of awareness that something special was happening. That she would catch a glimpse of Life itself. She then knew, truly knew, that she was an old soul. That she had been in this position many, many times before, and that her final act would be one of acute vigilance. To catch the last essence of Life as it was released from the body in which it travelled, and that if she concentrated her final energies, she too could be released from her form. Her energies reduced and reduced down to the smallest pulse. She would have to time it perfectly. The last fraction of a beat before the final pulse. If she could catch it just right. Just as her body slowed down and the Life left.

Wrinkles

Ocho called to his parents' house. When they asked about Ruth, he said that she was still away with work. They said she worked too hard. They said that if she had children she wouldn't be able to work so hard. They never said that about Ocho.

He didn't bring any meat this time. He had noticed that the meat he brought previously was still in his parents' freezer. The portions his parents ate were getting smaller and smaller. A pot of curry would last them a week instead of two days. After dinner, instead of chatting, his parents dozed on the couch with their mouths open. They must swallow a lot of spiders he thought. Their faces looked rubbery and tired. His father had more wrinkles than his mother, which he said was because he had worked outside all his life on the Stop/Go signs. His mother said his father wouldn't have so many wrinkles if he didn't sleep on his stomach with his face in the pillow.

Ocho couldn't concentrate on the TV. There was a European movie on that he had seen with Ruth. A meditation on grief and loss with a bit of sex in it. Ocho asked if he could sleep over. His parents were happy to have him staying under their roof. When Ocho checked in on them later to wish them a good night they were already out cold. They looked so small in their bed.

Ocho had a night of troubled sleep. The rat's brain was scurrying all over his life. His thoughts squirmed in his guts.

When Ocho woke up the next morning, he could hear his parents downstairs. They had the radio on loud as usual. It seemed that they listened to it louder these days. He kissed his mother on the forehead and patted his father on the shoulder. He asked them how they had slept, but they hushed him. Their attention was frozen by the story that was all over the news that morning. There had been a mass suicide among the Satanists at Ghost Mountain. A dozen of the Satanists were found dead, having choked on their own tongues. They had eaten poisoned herbs from Ghost Mountain or possibly overdosed on drugs.

His mother covered her mouth with her hand as she listened. His father paused with his spoon full of muesli before him. Only Ocho understood how the story affected them all. He was in shock. He could hardly feel his feet in his boots. His rat's brain fizzed and pulsed.

He kissed his parents and said he had to go to collect Ruth from the train station. They said to send their love and to tell her not to work too hard.

Once Ocho arrived home, he collapsed on the kitchen floor and doubled over with the cramps in his rat's brain. He squeezed his knees and cried. He wanted to know yet didn't want to know what he was already absolutely certain he knew.

Neighbours

The mass suicide on his land had scuppered any hope of the landowner becoming rich. Nobody would buy his property. It seemed to him that he had lost a fortune without having done anything. He truly did not understand money or land or power.

The week before, he had dropped a note in the door of his tenant inviting him for a stir fry. He had hoped they could discuss things like adults and come to some peaceful arrangement. Through the executrix, he had discovered that his tenant had stopped paying rent ever since his father had died many months before. He had planned to tell his tenant that he would forgive this debt, though he would not mention that he had spent the tenant's rental deposit.

However, the tenant had stood him up and the landowner ate his stir fry alone that night.

The landowner had been drinking his disappointment alone. He felt a lack of resolution in things. His father had died. He had failed as a landowner. There had been a mass suicide on his land. The police were involved and the whole thing was already becoming notorious. He went through the full sequence of drunkenness. Comfort, sorrow, self-pity, frustration, anger and self-righteousness. He resolved to visit his tenant. With nobody to advise him, the drink answered his logic.

He took a torch and walked out into the dark, starless evening. He rehearsed his points aloud as he walked along the unlit road.

In his drunkenness he banged on the door harder than he meant to. He realised that there were no lights on in the house.

He had no idea what time it was, except that it was certainly too late.

His tenant answered the door with his wife behind him, closing her dressing gown as she felt the cold air.

The landowner made his points loudly and incoherently. The fresh air had helped the alcohol sink into his brain. Strangely, even in the flow of this clownish performance there was a part of him that bore sober witness.

His mouth was open at the point of impact so his jaw took the full force, snapping his head. He fell onto the tarmac, landing on his side, and dropped his torch. He saw it flicker briefly before the batteries rolled down the driveway.

With nothing to light his way, he staggered along the country road, drunk and concussed. He couldn't remember whether he had taken the right or left from his tenant's house and couldn't tell whether he was getting closer to home or further away.

In the distance he saw what was either a motorbike or a car with only one headlight working. He stood in the middle of the road and waved it down. His jaw hung loose and useless and when he tried to call out, he could only croak something garbled. The car, as it turned out to be, seemed to slow as it approached him. And it did slow, but it didn't stop. The landowner's judgment of distance and time, and therefore speed, was as impaired as his judgment of everything else in his life.

The car hit him awkwardly along his left side, spinning him around and off into the ditch beside the road. There he collapsed, his limbs splayed and unresponsive. He was laid out with his head below the rest of his body, staring up at the night sky through his parted legs. His jaw hung loose like a swing. He could neither move nor make a noise. His windpipe was kinked by his posture and he could only breathe with difficulty. The pain was all that kept him awake.

Hours later, he was still lying there, immobile, when the sky warmed and brightened with the dawn. A bird he didn't know the name of approached and pecked at the ground around him.

It climbed onto his chest but he couldn't feel it. His exhaustion was replaced by hollow terror as he realised he couldn't feel his body.

In the calm clear morning, with the sounds of nature all around him, his last thought was how unusual it was to die that way, upside-down, suffocating with a bird resting in his open mouth.

Ashes

It took months for everything to get untangled. There were investigations and tests to establish the facts and apportion blame. None of it meant anything to Ocho. Ruth's body remained in State custody during that whole time. To them, she was nothing more than evidence.

Not only were the walkers thought of as Satanists but their bodies were considered satanic too. No religious facility would take them and put them to rest. Many of the families disowned them also. In the end, the State authorities cremated them. Ocho was given a shovel's worth of the resulting ashes in a metal box. The ashes may have been Ruth's or somebody else's or nobody's.

He took the ashes to Ghost Mountain, where he had spread his parents' ashes only a few months before. They had died without knowing what had happened to Ruth. He simply told them she had left him for a man named Carthage. They had become weaker and smaller since then. It had broken their hearts.

Ocho walked around Ghost Mountain clockwise and spread Ruth's ashes along the path, which was now overgrown. It was where she had been happiest and where he had been saddest. Anyone walking around the mountain would carry her ashes on their boots. She would continue to walk Ghost Mountain.

When the metal box was empty, Ocho walked back to the abandoned house where the old landowner and his missing son had lived, and where Ocho had been squatting since Ruth had died. His own house and his parent's house lay empty in every way. He could not say what strange gravity it was that kept him rooted there when everything about it gave him reason to catapult himself to the far side of the world away from it.

Ghost Mountain

Ghost Mountain had become a place where people no longer visited, no longer walked. Except for early mornings, when Elaine and Dominic and their child came to throw sticks for their dog, as the hares lay low in the grass.

BOOK 2

Ghost Mountain

In the years since everything had happened, the scar around the base of Ghost Mountain had healed. The ashes that were scattered there had been blown among the weeds or otherwise reborn among nature's infinite possibilities.

Ghost Mountain, as the scene of the tragedy, had also been implicated in its cause. People tended to stay away, but not for reasons they would admit. The remembering of what had happened there was left to those who couldn't forget. For everyone else, each new day brought new things to talk about and put the incident another twenty-four hours into the past.

But Ghost Mountain was not part of whatever happened or didn't happen. It had no relationship with time. There was a difference in materiality between Ghost Mountain and what was said about or associated with it. It was not possible to say what Ghost Mountain was or was not without the words failing or becoming unmoored from their meaning.

Ghost Mountain was not words.

Ghost Mountain was not the words "Ghost Mountain."

Ghost Mountain was Ghost Mountain.

Ocho

Ocho had never experienced grief until his parents and his wife died suddenly. Before then, he was only dimly aware of what grief was exactly. Nothing about the presence of Ruth and his parents in his life had prepared him for their absence.

To be precise, Ocho was experiencing three griefs. Each grief had its own characteristics.

The grief for his father was dulling. This reflected the fact that he and his father had a largely unexpressed relationship. That is not to say they weren't close, merely that they could spend time together and communicate without words. They recognised that much can flow between two people if you simply let it. Back and forth, a mutually sustaining flow. But this meant that the loss of his father was incommunicable. Without his father, there was no flow. Without flow there was stagnation. This is dulling grief. It sapped his appetites and sedated his instinct for social contact. This made it a long-form grief. It was the type of grief that a person often found hard to break alone.

The grief for his mother was based on warmth. Specifically, it is the warmth that supports a person or on which they lie. If the covers are swept from a sleeping child, they will complain about the cold. However, as their body feeds heat to the mattress beneath them, which will hold and return that heat, they will go back to sleep and have warm loving dreams. It is the warmth beneath them rather than the warmth above that makes the love in their dreams possible. But if the child tries sleeping on a cold floor with a warm blanket, they will end up with an unshakeable cold and loveless dreams. This is what losing his mother felt like to Ocho. She not only fed him love but held onto the love he gave her – preserved it – and fed it back to him. It was like when he lived at home and his mother demanded that he hand up half his wages as his contribution to the household expenses. He resented this at the time. When he moved out, his mother returned to him all the money he had handed up. The moral of that lesson was lost on him, but nevertheless his mother's love worked in the same way. All the love he had given her – including the love he expressed to her because it had nowhere else to go – she had minded for him until he needed it. This warmed his life. Since her death he simply could not get warm, no matter how many layers he added to his life. This is not the type of grief a person gets over. This type of grief you can only adapt to. You can never again find that sustaining warmth, the type of warmth you can sleep on. It then becomes your turn to store other people's warmth for them until they need it, but that comes much later. It comes much later because this is only possible once you are sure – in your mind and heart – that you know the difference between storing someone else's love and love that is yours.

Ocho's grief for Ruth was fundamentally different from anything he experienced for his father and mother. He and Ruth were like two sides of the same ladder. Her death was a sundering of the ladder down the middle. Holding one half of a ladder is in no way comparable to holding one side of a complete ladder. At every level of him, for each step, there was a counterpart that was missing. That is why a person suffering from this kind of grief can fall over.

It was true that all this knowledge was somewhere inside Ocho. But if you had stopped him in the street and asked him how his grief worked, you would not be talking to the part of Ocho that understood those things.

Elaine and Dominic and Ursula

Elaine and Dominic had a baby girl. They named her Ursula. Between them they were over one hundred years old when she was born. Neither had any ideas about parenthood and so they treated Ursula like another person in the house. They looked after her needs and gave her love, but they didn't act like they were the bosses or the presidents of her life. What do we know, they said. Elaine and Dominic were both estranged from their families. They both thought families were bullshit. But when the three of them were together it felt like love. Elaine didn't know if she loved Dominic – on account of the fact that he used to be the town drunk – but she loved the combination of Dominic, Ursula and her. Dominic was less complex. He loved Elaine and Ursula without any reason or strategy. Ursula liked her life with her parents. When she first started speaking they told her to call them Elaine and Dominic because they thought families were bullshit. They didn't want to use the vocabulary of families, or the vocabulary of bullshit, as they called it. But then, Dominic started having regrets when he heard other fathers being called Dad, Daddy and so on. He spoke to Elaine and she agreed that Ursula could call him "Captain." Ursula continued to call Elaine by her name.

They struggled for money. Elaine had a small pension, but it was not enough to support their household. Dominic was still self-employed but not self-paid, and theodolite work was hard to come by. He had worked briefly in the butcher's shop but Elaine didn't like him washing his clothes at home. She said she didn't want blood in the washing machine. She didn't want her clothes full of blood.

Elaine had hoped to make some money with her paintings but nobody wanted to buy them. She lacked faith in her work. Dominic tried to encourage her. He said they were haunting and that the main reason nobody bought them was because she only ever painted Dominic and Ursula and their dog on Ghost Mountain. Her pictures were too personal to sell, he said, despite being good enough. Elaine didn't think they were personal at all. How could paint be personal, she reasoned. She thought Dominic didn't understand art.

When Ursula was little they bought a pet Labrador. Elaine said that when she was a child, they had a Labrador and the kids had all learned to walk by holding on to the Labrador's coat. Labradors don't mind that stuff. It was painful for Elaine to get a new dog. She would never forget her dog that choked, Thelonious. They got the new dog from the pound and it was already a few years old, they didn't know how many years. It must have had a name before, but nobody knew what it was. It was impossible to guess. For days he went without a name. In the end, Dominic decided to call him Crabs. Ursula would often ask: "Captain – why is he called Crabs?" and Dominic would give her a different answer every time.

In the mornings, Dominic brought Crabs and Ursula for a walk on Ghost Mountain. Elaine stayed home and painted or had a nap. In the afternoons, they walked up Ghost Mountain together. It was always quiet up there these days.

By bedtime, everyone would be tired. Crabs was tired from running up and down Ghost Mountain. Ursula was tired from walking and from growing up. Elaine and Dominic were tired from looking after Ursula and worrying about money.

Though he was tired, Dominic would still get ideas in bed. Elaine didn't mind helping him with his ideas but, as far as she was concerned, she could live without that stuff. She would feel and caress his body and look at him as he squirmed and grimaced. And that's the way she painted Dominic. That's why he never looked right in her paintings.

Salt

Ocho often spent evenings and weekends at Ghost Mountain. It was not a grieving obsession. It was not so he could understand Ruth better. It was not so he could understand himself. Ocho seemed to be always in motion but at Ghost Mountain he was not in motion. He knew that an object will not change its motion unless a force acts upon it. He knew that when two objects interact, they apply forces to each other of equal magnitude and opposite direction. He didn't know whether he was a force or an object. He didn't know whether Ghost Mountain was a force or an object.

As he sat eating his lunch on a broken wall, he saw a young girl with her dog at the foot of Ghost Mountain. He had seen her and her family there many times before. He heard the town drunk ask her to wait while he emptied his bladder on the other side of Ghost Mountain. Ocho didn't initiate any talk. It was not good to talk to children. Children were taught not to speak to strangers. But the dog didn't understand. The dog came up and licked the fleshy part of his palm.

"He likes that," said the girl. "You must have salty hands."

Ocho did have salty hands from his lunch.

"What's his name?" he asked. "Or is it a she?"

"He's a he," she said.

The town drunk whistled as he came down the hill. The dog ran over to him with a carefree Labrador gait. The town drunk did a wave where he held up his hand but didn't wave it. Ocho did the same back, but to communicate he knew not what.

The dog jerked his head to the side and ran after something small, fast and brown that had moved in Ocho's peripheral vision. A leveret maybe. The town drunk called "Crabs! Crabs!" and took off after him, his daughter skipping behind.

Ocho had seen the town drunk and the town drunk's wife and the little girl walking on Ghost Mountain for years. Ever since Ruth had died and the little girl was a baby. Ocho sometimes filled in their story. The story of how the town drunk had a wife and a child that was more like a grandchild. What kind of person would want the town drunk as a husband, he wondered. What kind of person would want the town drunk as a father? Then he thought: I have no wife, I have no child, I have no grandchild, I have no dog. Whenever he had a thought like that, he noticed his posture. That his posture was slumped, as if gravity was too much for him. His posture was like that of a coat hung up. As he watched them walking up Ghost Mountain he heard the town drunk shouting at the girl not to throw a ball for the dog. That it was dangerous. The girl cried a little and then got angry. She threw the ball on the ground and the dog picked it up anyway. Ocho could feel himself judging the town drunk. Maybe if he wasn't the town drunk, Ocho would have thought differently. The town drunk was talking sweetly to the girl and apologising. Then they both started calling "Crabs! Crabs!"

There was an empty house near the foot of Ghost Mountain. It was where the landowner had lived briefly before he went missing. His father had lived there prior to that. Ocho had started staying there, though it smelled of rotten bananas. The lights still worked. Someone was paying the bills. He could hear scratching as he slept, which he thought was probably mice. It reminded him of the rat's brain in his gut. As he lay there he thought about Ruth. He missed her. He still felt like half a ladder and he missed Hee-Haw with her.

He licked his salty hand as he lay on his side. Not the hand the dog had licked, the other one. Nobody had touched him in so long. Only the dog. "Crabs! Crabs!" he called into the empty house.

He went to sleep with a salty taste in his mouth and the sweet smell of rotten bananas in his dreams.

School Sandwiches

Ursula started school. Her parents had sat on the edge of her bed and explained everything. There would be a teacher who would show her what to do and there would be other children her own age who would become her friends. She would learn lots of new and interesting things. It sounded good to Ursula. She told them she was looking forward to showing people her pictures of the three of them with Crabs at Ghost Mountain.

Then her parents explained that they wouldn't be there.

"Oh," she said.

"Why not?" she thought but didn't say.

Dominic and Elaine brought her to the door of her class. Her teacher had brown hair and glasses and spoke to Ursula like she was an idiot. Her parents always spoke to her like she was one of them, but the teacher didn't speak like that. The teacher also spoke to Dominic and Elaine like they were idiots. The teacher spoke about them like they weren't there.

"Mammy and Daddy have to go now," the teacher said.

How come she doesn't call them Dominic and Elaine, Ursula thought.

She sat at a hexagonal table on the smallest chair she had ever seen. The boy beside her was wearing a cowboy shirt and already eating his lunch. The girl on the other side of her was giggling with a similar-looking girl. They both had glitter on their nails. Ursula looked right and she looked left. These aren't going to be my friends, she thought. These children are idiots. Maybe that's why the teacher talks to people like they're idiots.

Ursula watched as different groups of parents dropped off children at the door and went through the same routine. All the parents looked so much younger than Dominic and Elaine.

At home, Elaine let Ursula paint whatever she wanted. But in school the teacher told them what to paint and made every child paint the same thing.

"Why?" thought Ursula.

After a few days of this, the boy to her right said to Ursula: "Where are your parents?"

Ursula said, "Captain and Elaine are my parents – they bring me to school every day."

"No," said the boy. "Those are your *grand*parents. That's why they are older than the other parents. You have to have parents too. You must have a mother and father somewhere."

Ursula thought about this. It made her feel like an idiot. How could a boy who ate his lunch at the start of the day make her feel like an idiot?

That evening she was quiet at the dinner table and didn't feel like drawing or painting. She looked at Dominic and Elaine across the kitchen and for the first time they looked like strangers. They looked so far away. All she could feel was the space between her and them. Where are my mother and father, she wondered? Is this why they never let me call them "mother" and "father"?

She rubbed some salt onto the thick part of her palm and got Crabs to come over and lick it off. It made her want to cry but she was angry and the anger trapped the hurt in her throat. She could hardly eat her mashed potato. It went cold in her mouth. When she eventually swallowed the mash it no longer tasted salty and creamy, like how Elaine always made it, but cold and compact like wet newspapers. Ursula imagined she was chewing the newspaper that had the news about her not having parents, only grandparents.

After dinner she found Elaine's hairbrush and pulled the loose hair from it. She lifted the hair to her nostrils to smell it but it only smelled of the rubber from the hairbrush.

That night, she called Crabs into her bed, though she wasn't allowed. He slept in a croissant shape, taking over the whole middle of the bed. Ursula curled herself around him and slept like that, making herself wheezy from the dog hairs.

The next morning at school, Ursula took the boy's lunchbox from the shelf quietly and put the hair from her mother's hairbrush in his sandwiches. She mushed it into the peanut butter or whatever it was. When the boy ate his lunch early as usual, he took several large bites at once and took further bites before swallowing what was already in his mouth. It took him a few moments to notice the difference in texture. Then he stopped and pushed his thumb and forefinger down his throat to pull out the wet clump of peanut butter and hair bread. He gagged as he was doing it. A bit of sick came down his nose. He shouted out "Teacher! Teacher!" and threw the congealed mess across the room. He panicked and started running around the hexagonal table. The other children laughed at him for being afraid of his own sandwiches.

It took a long time for the teacher to settle him down. He was hiccupping and crying. He kept wiping his nose on the sleeve of his cowboy shirt, so much so that he had to change into one of the art aprons instead.

Nobody really knew what had happened. Nobody suspected Ursula, who was quietly drawing a picture of herself and Dominic and Elaine and Crabs on Ghost Mountain.

Ursula knew of the word "sorrow" from the stories she had read with Elaine and for the first time in her young life she knew what it meant. It was worse than "sad" because sorrow was being sad and not being able to do anything about it. She had been sure that the hair sandwiches would make everything better, but the space between herself and Dominic and Elaine was greater than ever. So, she drew Dominic and Elaine and

Crabs all the way to the right of the page and drew herself all the way to the left, to see how far apart they truly were. It was very far. Much further than she had realised. It was so far that she could draw Ghost Mountain in its entirety in the gap.

Voice Message

Ocho was living a life of no stimulation. It was a non-life. At work, each day was a carousel of minor actions, each one nudging a task on to its next step but never starting or completing anything. He didn't even know who it was that started and finished the work that was always doing the rounds. All he knew was that when the work came his way he was supposed to catch it and pass it on, as if it were an errant frisbee in the park. Some years he was given a larger bonus and other years a smaller bonus. He did the same sort of work year after year, so the bonus was nothing to do with anything he did. It was to do with the market, his boss said, though his boss didn't exactly understand it either. His boss was an older man left over from an era when people didn't hassle their staff, so he didn't hassle Ocho in a good or bad way. He never told Ocho to work harder or differently but nor did he ask Ocho how he was or what he was interested in.

This is all a way of saying that Ocho was living a life of no stimulation. It was a non-life. Ocho didn't know whether this was because his parents and Ruth had died suddenly, leaving him in a state of stasis. Part of him thought that this is what his life would have been like had he never met Ruth. That this was all the life he deserved.

Ocho did not look in a mirror and realise anything profound nor did he have a breakdown. He did not take drugs or drink too much or shave his head or indulge in asceticism. Ocho did not analyse himself or chew on his emotions. Nor did he get a pet, though he sometimes wished he had a dog like Crabs.

Ocho could feel his connection to Ruth diminishing. The first thing he lost was her voice. He could not recreate the sound of her voice in his ears. He had only two of her voice messages on his phone. They were from a day when he had called her to complain that she was late. It pained him to listen to them. Why did I criticise my wife so much, he would ask himself. What was so important? He could hear in her voice how she felt criticised and accepted it. A voice that captured her sincerity towards him and his insincerity towards her. Why did I criticise my wife so much, he would again ask.

Not long after his parents died, Ocho found out that they hadn't been paying their mortgage. In fact, they hadn't paid it in years. He didn't know whether his father was supposed to take care of it, or whether they had both decided it was better to keep the money for themselves. Did they know they were dying, he wondered. While the woman from the bank had been explaining to him over the phone that the house was being repossessed, Ocho hadn't been paying attention. He had been drawing swirling designs on a notepad. It was a tattoo-shaped design. The woman from the bank had asked him if he understood, and he paused for a moment. Even though he was in the middle of losing something important, the thought of fighting for it exhausted him. "Oh, OK," he had said. The woman from the bank was friendly, almost joyful, after that. It must have been a conversation she was dreading. Afterwards, whenever Ocho thought about it, or when he saw someone with a swirling tattoo, it stung him. It stung him that his parents hadn't been able to pay their bills. The worry they must have carried stung him. The possibility that they knew they were dying for a long time and didn't tell him, stung him. The vaporising of his inheritance stung him. It made him want to stop paying his own half-mortgage. The other half was dead. It died with Ruth.

Sometimes when he was staying over at the abandoned rotten banana house at Ghost Mountain, he would sit in the armchair there and close his eyes to see if he could feel anything of Ruth. Whether any of her life energy was still abiding there. Ocho didn't believe in that stuff but he wanted to see whether it was true or whether he could make it true. He closed his eyes and imagined himself looking inside his head. Inside his body. Inside his bones. He looked inside himself where his organs were packed in. All the organs that would be too large and messy to fit back in there if they were ever to spill out. He tried to picture what the rat's brain in his gut looked like. In his mind it looked like a mess of tight wet grey knots. He could not find any trace of Ruth in there.

And then sometimes, when he was deeply lost, he would call: "Ocho! Ocho!" just like how the town drunk had called after Crabs. But his name would bounce off the bare walls and thin windows, echoing among the loneliness he himself had brought there.

Art Railings

Elaine decided to put her paintings up for sale. She would affix them to the railings around the park in town. She had seen other artists do this, both in the town and in other cities she had been to on holiday. She and Dominic needed the money, but the thought of selling the paintings filled her with doubt and sadness. With paintings, if she sold one, she would never see it again. She wished she was a writer or a musician instead, so that other people could enjoy her art without her having to relinquish it. It bothered her that someone else could own the paintings of her, Dominic, Ursula, Crabs and Ghost Mountain, that they could buy them even if they were a cruel or selfish person. The thought of a person like that looking at her pictures and licking their lips disgusted her.

She loaded her paintings into the boot of her car, each wrapped in one of her spare sheets, not that she had many to spare. When she ran out of sheets, she had to use some jumpers instead. She could hear the paintings sliding around as she turned corners. They clattered as she drove over speed bumps. The whole way there, she imagined them getting torn or damaged. Her doubting sadness became swollen inside her.

When she began affixing her paintings to a free space on the railings, another woman with paintings said she couldn't put them there. That spot was taken. Elaine found another space and asked the painter next to her if it was free or if another artist used it. The other painter said, in bad language, that she didn't much care what Elaine did.

So Elaine hung her paintings away from the others on a quieter corner of the park railings. It was a place of low footfall. It was apart from the other painters and apart from the atmosphere.

As she sat on a stool and waited she felt like she was being made to pull down her trousers and sit on the toilet in public. She felt humiliated and stupid.

Sometimes when she painted – the best times – she would feel a beautiful creative rain. Creative rain would shower her scalp and wash her whole body with light. Whenever she felt creative rain, she experienced neither time nor her own Elaineness. All she felt was a communion with her painting. It was not *her* creative rain. It didn't belong to anyone. It was hard to explain. When she looked at her paintings leaning against the wall at home, she could sense the creative rain that was in them. Her scalp tingled just looking at them. That's how she knew they were real paintings. She wondered whether people viewing them would be able to feel the creative rain too.

The creative rain was beautiful but it was easily overwhelmed by doubting sadness. As Elaine sat there looking at her paintings on the railings she felt only her doubting sadness.

A couple walked by and stopped at her pictures. They discussed her paintings as if she wasn't there. "They all look the same," the wife said. "The man's expression isn't quite right," said the husband. They walked on without acknowledging Elaine.

It was a long time before the next people came by. Elaine was getting cold and couldn't feel the soles of her feet. The next people were a young couple. "I like the dog in this one," said the young man. "There's a dog in all of them," said the young woman.

They turned to Elaine and asked her how much the paintings were selling for.

Elaine was sitting down and looking up at them. This made her feel even more like they were watching her going to the toilet. She had no business nous. She would have liked to have said: "Give me enough money so I don't ever have to do this again."

Instead, Elaine said a big number so that she wouldn't have to part with the painting.

"We have a dog like the one in the painting," said the man. "We have a little girl too. This painting looks like our family."

Elaine wasn't sure if this meant they were negotiating.

"What's your dog called?" asked Elaine.

"Thelonious," said the young woman, or at least that was the name Elaine heard.

"That was my old dog's name," said Elaine. Her doubting sadness was joined by a familiar grieving sadness.

Elaine let them have one of the smaller paintings for a small number.

After they left, Elaine stacked the pictures back into the boot of her car with the sheets and the jumpers. Driving home, she could hardly feel the car pedals with the cold soles of her feet.

Elaine could feel doubting sadness, grieving sadness and then the ordinary sadness she felt whenever she was emotionally tired. It interested her that her heart could hold such different flavours of sadness at the same time without them mixing.

The whole way home she could feel the absence of the missing painting. She had always been sensitive to absences.

Front Teeth

Dominic had never been employed before. He had only ever been self-employed. The problem was that he was seldom self-paid. He found money elusive. It had abstract qualities that he didn't understand.

In the years since becoming parents, money had been a worry for Elaine and Dominic. Now that Ursula had started school, they began to notice that she stood out among her classmates. Her clothes were too big or too small and had been washed too many times. This made her look like she had been washed too many times also.

Though they both hated family bullshit and other conforming bullshit, they were concerned that it would be Ursula and not they who would bear the burden of their principles. Ursula's teacher had phoned one day to say that Ursula had broken into sobs when the class was asked to write an essay titled "My Parents." Elaine and Dominic were hurt by this.

Dominic decided to apply for jobs. He wrote job letters in longhand to a few places. Even though he had little experience, and his hands shook from years of drinking, he had beautiful handwriting. The man who ran the heel bar read his letter and was impressed by its curlicue elegance. The man rang and said to "drop in for a chat." Then he clarified, "It's not an interview. We tend to keep it casual around here." Dominic liked the sound of that.

It was a Saturday morning and Ursula was still asleep. She was wiped out after a long week at school. School was so much more exhausting than being at home with Elaine. Ursula slept on her stomach with her arms and legs stretched out like a starfish. Dominic leaned over to kiss the back of her head and sang, "Good morning, little Ursula." Ursula woke with start and jerked her head back. She smashed Dominic in the mouth. Ursula shouted out "Ow, ow, ow, OW!" Dominic shouted many loud curses he had forgotten he knew. His mouth pumped with blood and he spat his two front teeth into his hand.

Ursula thumped his arm with her fists for hurting her. She touched the back of her head and screamed when she saw blood on her fingers from the cut in her scalp. "You bit me, Captain, you bit me!" she remonstrated.

Even though he was angry at her and even though it grossed him out to rub his tongue along the gap in his gums and taste the blood, he still comforted her and apologised and said it was OK.

He had blood on the front of his shirt and also on the back where Ursula had hugged him with blood on her fingers.

"Look," he said, to cheer her up.

He held out his two front teeth on the palm of his hand. They looked long, like horse's teeth.

Ursula's jaw went slack. She was calm all of a sudden.

"Can I have them?" she asked.

"Why not. They're no use to me anymore."

Elaine was out selling her pictures, so Dominic would have to bring Ursula with him to the informal chat that wasn't an interview at the heel bar. Ursula held his hand as they walked there. She gripped the teeth in her other hand, checking them every few minutes. Dominic was missing his front teeth and had blood soaked into his shirt. He was glad that it was just an informal chat and not an interview.

The man at the heel bar was not expecting this.

"What happened to you?" he asked.

Dominic explained. He asked Ursula to show the man the teeth.

"You need to put those in a cup of milk and bring them to a dentist straight away," said the man.

Ursula looked at Dominic.

"I have already said she could have them," said Dominic.

"But they're your front teeth," said the man. "And you've lost a lot of blood."

"Will that count against me for the job?" asked Dominic.

The man dropped to his haunches and tried to talk Ursula into giving up the teeth, but it was no use.

"Do I get the job?" asked Dominic.

"How can you work with all that blood on your shirt and with a dental emergency and with your child here too?"

Dominic could see why he had remained self-employed for all these years.

"OK, thanks anyway," said Dominic. Where was he going to get money now? He was disappointed for himself and for his family.

"But hey," said the man, "Let me get you a new shirt. I'll have a look in the staff room. Maybe we can talk about a job some other time?"

The man left through the back of the shop and Dominic took off his blood-stained shirt. He held it up and realized he would not have hired someone wearing it either. He and Ursula sat on heel bar stools and waited, looking at all the unusual equipment for fixing heels and cutting keys. It would have been a great place to work. Dominic rubbed his gums with his tongue. Ursula stroked the teeth with her thumb. Each had something to remind them of the other.

Ghost Mountain

Ocho was spending more and more time at Ghost Mountain, in the rotten banana house.

On weekday evenings it would already be dark when he arrived, after work, with his overnight bag. The lights were working. Someone was still paying the bills. This meant that it was still someone else's house. It meant that it was not his house. This was both good and bad. It was good because it meant that he wasn't getting sucked into Ghost Mountain the way Ruth had been. But it was bad because Ghost Mountain was the only place he wanted to be these days. His own house had become a widower's house. It held too much of Ruth and her absence was everywhere. Ruth would often buy small things for the house whenever they had money to spare. Ornaments, kitchen gadgets, pictures. He had always said he didn't like them. That they cluttered the place or that he had been hoping to use the money for something else. He would say that it was OK but next time she should talk to him first because it was their shared money. Why had he done this, he wondered. Why did he criticise his wife so much?

Whenever he spent a weekend at the rotten banana house, he would wake early, when there were not yet any words in his brain. He would sit on the cracked cold wall outside and watch how the sunrise cast its light on Ghost Mountain. It was different every day. The light travelled invisibly through the air but when it hit Ghost Mountain it would resolve into a yellowy light, a blue light or a grey light. It had other qualities too – grainy light, light with definition, light without definition, restless light, stable light. As Ocho observed this, these descriptions would suggest themselves to his wordless brain.

The vegetation on Ghost Mountain was patchy and uninteresting. Low grasses, thick-stalked briars, gorse, weedy flowers. It had spread like a few days' beard about halfway up the slopes. There were some butterflies and wasps which meant that whatever they fed on was there also. And of course, midges.

He had seen leverets, though he had not yet seen one carried off – alive or dead – by the buzzards that hovered in the eddies above the mountain.

While he hadn't seen any, he assumed there were mice or rats everywhere.

But Ocho was not interested in the nature on Ghost Mountain. The names of things or their habits meant nothing to him. Ghost Mountain was Ghost Mountain. He could not find Ruth there. He wondered whether he was seeing what she had seen. He had been stupid to have scattered her ashes there, as if it were possible for her to become part of Ghost Mountain. He had been stupid to scatter his parents' ashes there – they who had never been to Ghost Mountain. He wished he could go up on the slopes with tweezers and retrieve every last flake of ash.

Ocho saw the town drunk and his family arrive to walk up Ghost Mountain, as they often did. They were usually running with their dog but today only Crabs was enthusiastic. The town drunk looked tired and his wife looked tired. The child was lagging behind them and they had to stop every few minutes. Ocho looked at the town drunk and reflected on how life changes so much for some people that they have to become different people. He wondered whether he too would ever have a second wife, a first child and a dog. He would have to become a different Ocho for any of that to be possible. He was between Ochos. He wasn't yet a new Ocho but he was also uncoupled from the Ocho he had been, the Ocho that had lived his memories. His memories felt like a bag of dirty laundry. He hadn't opened the bag in the years since Ruth died. This is because once he opened it, he would have to sort through it. He did not have the strength for that. The part of him that was in the laundry bag of memories would have to remain inaccessible. A large part of the Ocho that used to live inside him, was now in that bag.

He returned to looking at Ghost Mountain and listening to the town drunk calling after Crabs. The town drunk was trying to whistle with his fingers in his mouth but he couldn't make his usual sound.

Jawbone

Ursula lagged behind her parents. There was a gap between them. There was a gap between them because she lagged behind but also because they were more like her grandparents and she was missing the parents who should have been between her and Dominic and Elaine. This gap was painful for her to think about. Whenever she looked at the gap in Dominic's mouth, where his front teeth had been, she thought about the gap in her family.

Ursula held on to the two missing teeth like they were her two missing parents.

One tooth was her mother and one tooth was her father. The father tooth had a chip in it and was a little yellow. The mother tooth was perfect. She played with them on her pillow and talked to them. When Crabs came into her bed, she pretended that he was Crabs Mountain and that the mother tooth and the father tooth were walking with her up his hairy back. She loved to climb Crabs Mountain with her teeth parents.

Compared to that, walking on Ghost Mountain with Dominic and Elaine was an empty experience. She used to gambol around after Crabs but now all she could feel was the heaviness of the boggy ground, the steepness of the gradient and the cold foggy air that gave her earaches. Crabs kept bringing her the tennis ball. It was wet with his saliva. She flung it into the ground instead of throwing a high underarm throw, the way he liked. She wasn't mad at Crabs, but he was tied up in her loneliness so she took it out on him. "Stupid Crabs" she would say when he retrieved the ball and waited for her to throw it, looking at her like she was his best friend.

In school, when she was having lunch in the playground, the children started talking about their families and whose father was the strongest and whose mother was the most beautiful. Nobody picked Dominic or Elaine. When he came to collect her from the school gates, she said "Captain – why are you such a weakling?" and ran on ahead of him. At dinner, when Elaine told her not to pour salt on her hand for Crabs to lick, she shouted "Why are you so old and ugly – nobody likes you!" then ran up to her room. She had already fallen asleep by the time Elaine came up to comfort her. Ursula was holding mother tooth and father tooth in her fist.

Ursula thought about running away, but she didn't know how to.

Ursula thought about moving into the house on Ghost Mountain, but there was already a man staying there. Dominic said the man's wife had been killed by Ghost Mountain. This scared her.

So, Ursula carried on doing the only thing she knew how to do, which was to be unhappy.

When they left Ghost Mountain they walked back home along the road. Dominic and Elaine stopped every once in a while to wait for her or to tell her to step in from the road if a car was coming. Ursula was dragging a big stick on the road. Crabs was hanging back with Ursula. She threw the tennis ball for Crabs and it rebounded off a low branch into the ditch. Crabs went in after it. When he came out, his legs and stomach were brown up to the water line. Crabs had found a stick. Ursula took the stick from his mouth. It had a crack in it. It had teeth. It was a jawbone. Ursula swished it in a puddle of clean water and dried it with some grass. She put it in her pocket. The opposite pocket to where she kept mother tooth and father tooth.

"Ursula!" called out Elaine. "Car coming! Stand in!"

Ursula stood sideways. She felt the wind from the car as it passed. She closed her eyes and imagined the car hitting her jaw and her two front teeth flying out.

Crabs pushed his nose into her pocket. He had lost interest in the tennis ball. He only wanted her to throw the jawbone.

Mandible

Dominic rolled off Elaine and lay on his back. They both preferred coupling in the morning when they were more rested. At night they fell asleep quickly and deeply. Their bodies were spent long before they got to bed. In the morning, they sometimes woke to some small allotment of energy that Dominic liked to spend carnally. Elaine would have preferred sleeping, but if it made Dominic happy she was OK to go along with it. He squirmed and grimaced as he lay on top of her. She could see the gap in his teeth as his mouth hung open. It disgusted her a little, but no more so than any other aspect of it all.

As Dominic breathed heavily beside her, she gathered up her nightclothes and straightened the bed. She got dressed and made Ursula's breakfast. While Dominic dozed upstairs, she tidied up her brushes and art materials. She had too many paintings, but all she could think about was the painting she had sold. She ached for it.

At the school she felt awkward around the other parents, who were much younger and all networked to each other somehow. She watched Ursula standing in the line for her class. A few children had the same coat as Ursula, which made Elaine feel like she was finally getting things right.

None of this came naturally to her. She didn't enjoy the business of making babies. She didn't have any insight into parenthood, except that she didn't want a family like the one she had grown up in. Her family with Dominic and Ursula was now what she thought of when she said "family." If people said: "How is your family?" she would answer with respect to

Dominic and Ursula, not the family she had grown up in and become estranged from.

One of the mothers had asked Elaine whether she worked. Elaine didn't want to say she was retired. She felt self-conscious about her age. She said she was a painter. The mother asked her what she painted and Elaine said portraits. The mother said she hoped they weren't nudes, and then laughed. But Elaine didn't laugh. Elaine wanted to say to the woman: you're a mother, you have children – how did you make them with your clothes on? But instead she said that it was more of a hobby.

Ursula's teacher arrived to bring the children into the classroom. Elaine saw the teacher asking Ursula something, and then Ursula turned and pointed to Elaine.

The teacher was smiling as she came towards Elaine. Elaine didn't know whether to stand and make the teacher do the walking or meet her halfway.

The teacher smiled hello and addressed her as Mrs Dominic's surname.

She asked Elaine about the mandible that Ursula had brought in for the classroom nature table. Was it a human mandible? she asked. Was it real? It looked real, she said.

Elaine wasn't certain what a mandible was. She knew it was a bone, maybe a jawbone, but she wasn't sure enough to say. She said she knew nothing about it.

In the end, the police got involved. Ursula showed them where Crabs had found it in the ditch. It was the jawbone of the landowner who had gone missing. They found the rest of the landowner's remains there too.

The local newspaper said that the town drunk (58) and the woman who had fought for a right of way (59) were involved but they were not suspects. The remains had been found by their granddaughter, Una.

Afterwards, nobody at school would play with Ursula because she had touched a dead body. They said that anyone who touched Ursula would get Ursula's disease, and die.

Searching for Ocho I

As Ocho watched Ghost Mountain from the cracked cold wall outside or sat staring at it emptily from the old chair inside the rotten banana house, he carried with him the thought about what it meant to be between Ochos. The Ocho he had been all those years felt so far away, and so inextricable from the memories he was avoiding, yet no new Ocho opened up before him.

He called out in the rotten banana house: "Ocho! Ocho!"

His name rebounded from the bare walls and the thin windows.

He looked out at Ghost Mountain.

He closed his eyes and let the name "Ocho" reverberate around his body.

The name was like a rubber ball that ricocheted around the empty space behind his forehead, where his thoughts were meant to be, and down into his chest cavity where his feelings were meant to be.

He repeated the name: "Ocho! Ocho!" and once again followed it around his body, like a rubber ball.

Throughout the day, his name bounced around inside him, without ever colliding with anything that could be considered "Ocho."

He slept deeply each night.

The name "Ocho" bounced around his dreams.

Searching for Ocho II

Within his body, there was one area untouched by his name.

The "Ocho" never reverberated in the rat's brain in his gut. Nothing came back from there. Any "Ocho" he sent there became lost in the dense tangle of tight wet grey knots. The "Ochos" he sent there died.

He concentrated on sending "Ocho" after "Ocho" into the rat's brain in his gut.

He assaulted his rat's brain with "Ochos" like radiation therapy.

But the rat's brain could not be penetrated. He could not use the name to find his way in there.

Whenever he was in the rotten banana house, or when he went walking around Ghost Mountain, he would bark the "Ochos" he was firing into his rat's brain.

He wished he had someone to teach him how to do it properly.

He wished he had someone to tell him whether it was the right thing to do.

He worried that his mind was eating itself and making his name eat his body.

"Ocho" he would call urgently, sending the name into his rat's brain as if zapping space invaders in a video game.

But the rat's brain absorbed it all.

Ocho called to Ruth for help: "Ruth, what should I do?"

Ruth said, "Hi Ocho!"

"I wish you could help me," he said.

"Of course," she said.

"What am I supposed to do?" he asked.

"What are you trying to do?" Ruth asked.

"I'm trying to shoot "Ochos" into the rat's brain in my gut."

"I see," she said.

"The "Ochos" echos around my empty insides and then die in the rat's brain of my gut – is that what's supposed to happen?" he asked.

"I can't tell you anything you don't already know," she said.

"Why not?" he asked.

And then he knew.

She was a Ruth he had summoned from his imagination.

He could tell by the voice.

It wasn't Ruth's voice from the voice message he had kept and he was unable to make her say new things.

And so he tried to summon his parents instead.

But all he could summon was an image of them sleeping.

They looked so serene that he could not bear to disturb them. He loved them too much to wake them.

Searching for Ocho III

Ocho slept, slept, slept.

He was between Ochos. He had abandoned or been abandoned by the old Ocho but there was no new Ocho ready for him to be.

He felt sad for the Ocho he had lost. He wanted to take care of it. It had been many Ochos. It was all the Ochos he had ever been. He wanted to take care of them. He did his best to nurse and comfort them before firing them into his rat's brain.

For so long he had been those Ochos. Ridding himself of them felt like dying.

For so long he had identified with those Ochos, and now their death felt like his death.

One morning, he called "Ocho" and nothing came up. No more Ochos.

Just the word, "Ocho."

He fired the word into his rat's brain but it had gone.

The tangle of tight wet grey knots had loosened itself.

He went to summon the "Ochos" from where his rat's brain had been, but no Ochos came up. Only the words. When he tried to fire the words, they stayed in his mouth.

Ocho walked around the rotten banana house.

He felt different.

He went out on to Ghost Mountain.

He stood on the summit and asked, "Did you do this?"

But Ghost Mountain was Ghost Mountain.

There were no answers for Ocho.

Ocho could not solve Ghost Mountain and he could not solve himself.

He was wasting his time there.

He packed up his overnight bag and returned to his widower's house. He wanted to see what was left of himself when he was without Ghost Mountain, and when he was without all the Ochos he had ever been.

Christopher

Ursula had been going to school and coming home without ever telling Elaine and Dominic that she had been ostracised or that she felt a deep gap in her life where her parents were meant to be. It was strange to her how easy it was to keep things from them. It was addictive in a perverse way. Like holding her breath. Each extra second of withholding the information felt like a new record. The longer it went on the harder it would be to beat her new record and so she kept on not telling them. As they didn't notice what they weren't looking out for, this pattern soon became normal.

At school, among her classmates, whatever she touched would become ostentatiously tainted. The girls at her table moved their chairs away from her. The boy beside her refused to share the paintbrush she had touched. When she sat down on the bench to have her lunch, the other kids would get up and scream that they had narrowly escaped infection with Ursula's disease.

Ursula didn't know whether they hated her because she had touched the jawbone of a dead man or whether they had always hated her and were glad to have the jawbone excuse on which to hang their hatred. She didn't like them or crave their friendship and yet their rejection ate her confidence. Because she didn't know how things worked and didn't understand her life, she joined them in their attitude and started hating herself.

She would put stones in her shoes when she walked.

She would make deliberate mistakes in her homework and spelling tests.

She would push her sandwiches into the gutter and go hungry.

She would bite her nails too short.

One day there was a new boy at school. He was a lot bigger than the other children and looked like he was a couple of years older.

The teacher told him to sit next to Ursula. The only free seats were the two seats either side of her.

The teacher asked him to stand up and tell the class a little about himself.

He said his name was Christopher.

He said his mother had been his teacher at home but now he had to go to school like everyone else.

He said he didn't want to be here.

He said he didn't know where his father was.

He said that his father wouldn't get lost because his father used to be the Clerk of Maps.

He said his mother is the smartest teacher there is.

He said they had moved into the house of a guy who had died.

He said they lived beside a mountain.

He said he knew loads of bad words but he wasn't allowed to say them in school.

He said he didn't want to make friends.

He said that when his father returned he would beat up all the other fathers.

The teacher told him he could sit down, so Christopher sat down. He took out a fistful of crayons and started drawing chaotic pictures.

Ursula stared at him.

"Stop looking at me," he said without lifting his eyes from his page. He kept drawing. His picture looked like a big fire, though the colours he used weren't fire colours.

The next day, Christopher's mother came to the school with him. She had beautiful corkscrew curls and looked more vivid than anything else in the room. She gave the teacher a bunch of letters, which the teacher distributed to all the children in the class, including Ursula. They were to bring the letters home to their parents, but most of the kids opened them on the avenue while walking home from school. The letters were an invitation to a "Friendship Party" at Christopher's house. The girls who opened them screamed as if the invitations had Ursula's disease. They tossed them into the bushes. The boys didn't do this because they were intimidated by Christopher on account of his size and his threat towards their fathers.

Ursula handed the letter to Dominic, like she was supposed to.

"Who's Christopher?" he asked.

"Some new kid at school," said Ursula, pretending to draw, but deeply interested in what Dominic would think.

"Why did he invite you to his party?" he asked. "Is he a new friend?"

"Everyone got one," Ursula said, without looking up. She had bitten her nails too short and it hurt when she held the crayon tightly. She let it hurt her.

Dominic brought Ursula to the party. She was wearing a new but simple dress and carrying some paintbrushes and paints as a present for Christopher. Ursula couldn't believe that Christopher lived in the house at Ghost Mountain. He and his mother had moved in that week and there were boxes and boxes of stuff everywhere. Christopher's mother was baking or cooking but none of the baking or cooking was ready. She hadn't put drinks out and there were no balloons and there was no music. Dominic and Ursula sat on the two hard chairs that were left out. They perched on the edge and fidgeted with their fingers.

Christopher's mother didn't apologise or make excuses or do any of the other things people do when they are hosting parties.

After a while, Dominic said: "We've met before. Your husband is the Clerk of Maps. I used to work with him"

"I remember, though he *was* my husband and he *was* the Clerk of Maps," she said, as she crouched to check on whatever was in the oven. The smell escaped. It was like meat and salt and oil.

Dominic glanced at Ursula.

"You can go out and play with him if you want, Angela," said Christopher's mother to Ursula.

Ursula looked at Dominic, who nodded to her to go ahead.

She approached Christopher uncertainly. He was banging a large stick against the bar of the rusty front gate. Sometimes it made a ringing sound and other times a dead sound, depending on whether he struck a hollow or solid section. He was absorbed in it, so Ursula didn't want to disturb him. His cheeks were flushed red and his fringe was sweaty.

"Why are you always staring at me?" he asked.

"I'm here for your party," she said.

"What party?"

"The party on the invitation."

Christopher stopped the clanging and looked at her.

"What are you talking about? It's not my birthday."

He leaned on the stick. He looked like a grown man, only smaller.

"The Friendship Party," said Ursula. "The teacher gave us all invites."

Christopher flung the stick away without looking where it landed and stormed into the house.

"Shit in a bag!" he shouted at his mother. Ursula heard slamming of doors.

Ursula wondered whether she was in trouble.

When she went back in, Christopher's mother was leaning with her backside on the countertop a little bit. Dominic was standing in front of her with his arms crossed. There wasn't much room between them.

"Looks like there's no party after all, kiddo" said Christopher's mother.

Dominic's eyes were on Christopher's mother, but he snapped out of it when Ursula took his hand.

Dominic brought her home.

"Christopher's mother said you could keep the paints and the brushes," he said.

Ursula thought about Christopher on the way home. She thought about Dominic standing close to Christopher's mother. She thought about how Christopher's mother was the right age for a mother. She thought about how she might adopt Christopher's mother as her own mother, to fill the gap. That would make Christopher her new brother. She wondered about whether that was possible.

But mostly she giggled to herself as she thought about the words "Shit in a bag!"

Brother

The next day at school, Christopher sat in his usual seat beside Ursula and started drawing his fire pictures without using fire colours. He was calm and quiet and acted like he had never met Ursula before. Ursula was disappointed. She wanted to make a joke with him about "Shit in a bag." The teacher was letting the children entertain themselves while she corrected homework at the top of the class. The children were chatting in their groups, none of which included Ursula or Christopher. Nobody was talking about Christopher's non-party.

Ursula looked at Christopher, thinking of him as a brother figure. He was big and his body was soft but his face was serious with concentration and also another type of seriousness. It was like the seriousness that adults have. His drawings were childish though, even for a kid his age. They didn't look like anything. When he was drawing them he looked serious but the pictures didn't look serious. Ursula thought about what she wanted from a brother. She wanted someone bigger than her. Big enough to fill some of the gap where her parents were meant to be. The way Christopher drew his pictures, it was like he had some sort of gap too. Perhaps the gap was the father who he said was away and would beat up all the other fathers when he returned.

"Stop staring at me," he said, without looking up from his picture.

The boy who always ate his sandwiches early was eating his sandwiches. He walked over to Christopher and started speaking with his mouth full.

"I told my father about you," the boy declared, "and he said he would break your father's jaw, and that you are to tell your father that."

Christopher looked at the boy without reacting. Looked at him as if he were something boring the teacher had written on the whiteboard. Ursula could tell that the boy had built up to this moment and had been bracing himself for a reaction. The boy drew his arm back and punched Christopher in the chest. It was as though the boy had punched a sack of cement. Christopher didn't flinch or move or in any way register the impact of the puny punch. The boy had skinned his knuckle on one of the buttons on Christopher's shirt. The boy looked at his knuckle and then started sucking it. The boy sat down and alternated between taking a bite from his sandwich and sucking his knuckle. Sometimes he sucked his knuckle while he still had food in his mouth.

Christopher went back to his drawing.

Ursula thought that if she were Christopher – and if she were Christopher's size – she would have emptied the boy's schoolbag and stuffed him head-first into it and then zipped up the bag and carried him around on her back all day as a punishment. But Christopher did nothing.

"Stop staring at me," he said, without looking up from his picture.

"Aren't you angry?" asked Ursula. "Aren't you going to fight him or something?"

"Who?" asked Christopher.

"Him," said Ursula, pointing to the boy, who had finished his sandwiches and was wiping his fingers on his trousers.

Ursula stormed up to the boy and slapped him in the face. The boy stared at her. The children stopped talking and stared with their mouths open. The teacher hadn't seen what had happened. She looked up from her desk and told the children to settle down. The boy's cheek started to redden. The redness on his cheek was the shape of Ursula's hand.

Ursula sat back down.

"Shit in a bag," said Christopher under his breath.

Ursula then realised that "Shit in a Bag," was not meant to be funny. It was serious. Just like Christopher.

Ursula decided that if Christopher was going to live on Ghost Mountain and she was going to go walking on Ghost Mountain, and if she had Ursula's disease and he as good as had Ursula's disease, then she might as well do something to show everyone that she and Christopher were together.

She reached over and took Christopher's fire picture from him.

"Why don't you use fire colours?" she asked.

"It's not a fire," he said.

"Then what is it?"

"It's the mountain near where I live."

"It doesn't look like a mountain," said Ursula.

"I didn't say it *looked* like the mountain."

Ursula didn't understand but sort of did understand at the same time. She put the picture in her bag without asking Christopher if she could have it.

To Ursula, this meant that he had accepted her proposal to be her brother.

Portrait

Elaine was trying to paint Dominic's portrait again. In her other pictures of him the likeness still wasn't quite right. This was partly because her painting was haunted by the squirming grimace of his lovemaking, made worse by his now missing front teeth. But there was something else. Something unresolved that was trying to figure itself out inside her. Painting always prompted Elaine towards unresolved things.

Dominic's suffered from restlessness. Even when he sat still, his eyes sought out distraction. He was especially restless today. Like he had somewhere else to be. But restlessness was not easy to paint. Elaine sat with the problem. She thought that maybe his posture would convey his restlessness. But her real problem was the face, not the body. If she painted him close-up, the gap in his teeth would steal the painting. People would call this the painting of the gap-toothed man. That was not what was unresolved inside her and not what she needed to paint.

Elaine thought about his squirming grimace. She had not known sexual intimacy in her life before she slept with Dominic. For over fifty years she had lived without it and without interest in it. She had assumed it would not form part of her life. It had happened at a time when she was vulnerable because she was grieving for her dog, Thelonious, who had choked. Dominic was kind about it, and he was vulnerable then too, so her guard was down. The squirming grimace was a curiosity for her then. A detail. A moment when she thought, OK, so this is what it's like. And then they had Ursula together, and the squirming grimace became associated with something beautiful. Complicated but beautiful. And lifechanging. But the squirming grimace wasn't always so significant. Sometimes it was just Dominic relieving himself. Relieving himself inside her.

"Is everything OK?" asked Dominic. "You're not doing much painting."

"I'm thinking," she said. "It's like this at the start."

She had almost forgotten he was there. She had been considering him as an art object. Now she switched to considering him as a love object. She looked inside herself to locate her Dominic love and to consider its tones, its colours, its lines, so that she could paint it. When she looked for it, though, she found that it was next to her love for Ursula. Her love for Ursula had turned into a sad love because of Ursula's remoteness. It hurt Elaine to love Ursula, and the more it hurt, the more she loved her, which made Elaine hurt all the more. On the other side of her Dominic love was her grief-love for Thelonious, her dog who had choked. Her grief-love was unexpressed because she felt stupid about missing her dog. Once they got Crabs it probably seemed to everyone that Crabs had replaced Thelonious. But one dog can't replace another, the same way one person cannot replace another.

It was impossible for her to separate these loves. It was like trying to divide a balloon.

Elaine worked away on the physical Dominic. She began sketching his shapes and took some pictures of him on her phone. She recreated his geometry. This was painting him technically. This was not how she resolved things but was a preliminary step. Like sanding a surface before varnishing it. As she worked, the creative rain prompted her towards what remained unresolved.

She sensed him tiring. She could feel his energy draining and it began to drain the energy of the picture. His restlessness had made him bored.

She asked Dominic to open his eyes a little.

"Sorry," he said. "Sorry."

"Maybe that's enough posing for today," she said. "I have pictures I can work from."

Dominic rubbed his eyes and did a waking-up yawn, which was different to a falling asleep yawn. He came towards her to see what she had done, but she said, "Don't. It's not ready. It's barely started."

Dominic tried to whistle for Crabs but couldn't because of his missing teeth, so he called the dog instead. He was always forgetting and then being reminded about his teeth. He called Ursula too.

Crabs bounded towards Dominic, excited about his leash.

Ursula came down the stairs unenthusiastically. She didn't respond to Elaine when she called "Hey Ursula!" in a friendly voice. Ursula's remoteness filled the house. It filled Elaine.

Dominic said that the Clerk of Map's wife, or the ex-Clerk of Map's ex-wife, had started renting the house at Ghost Mountain. He said her name was Martha and that he was going to return the theodolite to her. It was rightfully hers, he said. And, after all, it had been lying against the wall in the spare room all this time. Dominic leaned in and kissed Elaine goodbye on her cheek which she lifted up to him. He had forgotten about not coming too close to the painting.

Ursula didn't say goodbye and her remoteness remained in the house even after she had left.

Dominic is bringing that woman the theodolite, thought Elaine. She understood what that meant. Dominic was a man of crushes. He had told her about the crushes of his childhood. Elaine had been his crush and now this new woman was probably his new crush.

Elaine continued to work on the painting. She tended it, like it was a fire that needed to burn out.

Later, when Dominic returned, he had wine on his breath.

Sit-Ups

Whenever Dominic brought Ursula to see Christopher, Martha would send them out to play while she and Dominic talked.

Outside, Christopher would ignore Ursula and go around striking sticks off various things to see what they sounded like, or else he would dig a hole.

Ursula would watch him and ask things like "What are you doing?" "Why are you doing that?" "Why won't you answer me?"

This time he was striking a stick off a rock at the foot of Ghost Mountain to see what it would take to break it. The stick was tougher than he expected and split without breaking. He sucked a splinter from his thumb and said, "Shit in a bag."

"Did you get a splinter?" asked Ursula. "Do you want me to take it out?"

Christopher ignored her as usual.

"Do you think Captain is going to marry your mother?" she asked.

Christopher returned to bashing his stick.

"That would make you my brother," she added.

Christopher stopped and looked at her. He winked at the sun behind her.

"I already have a father," he said. "Nobody can switch him for another father. And nobody is going to be my mother's husband except for my father. Got it?"

Ursula chewed his answer. He spoke with such certainty. It made her doubt herself. It took her a moment to recalculate what was what.

"Why do you call him Captain anyway?" he asked. "Is he not your real father?"

Ursula gave him a cold look, and stroked Dominic's front teeth in her pocket. She reached over and grabbed Christopher's stick and threw it away. It helicoptered over some rocks behind him. It left behind a splinter in the slack between her thumb and forefinger. She would have sucked it had Christopher not been watching.

Christopher stomped off up Ghost Mountain.

Ursula usually walked around Ghost Mountain rather than climbing it. She was a little afraid of the summit because it was high, though not very high, and also because Ghost Mountain had so many stories told about it.

She followed him up reluctantly.

Christopher reached the summit quickly and easily. He stood up there with a conquering stance.

"Sometimes, when I fight with my mother, I run up here to see what I can see," said Christopher. "To see if I can see my father coming."

He looked at Ursula to check her reaction, then turned again to look out over the landscape.

"Shit in a bag," he said quietly.

Ursula looked up at him. Her hair had blown out of her clips and was whipping her eyes.

"Want to see how strong I am?" he asked.

Without waiting for Ursula to answer he sat down in front of her with his legs straight out.

"Hold my ankles."

Ursula held them and he started doing sit-ups.

"I can do twenty," he said through gritted teeth.

Ursula counted aloud as he lifted himself up with his hand behind his head.

When he had reached twenty he looked at her to see if she was impressed.

"It's easy doing them downhill. Let's swap places and see if you can do them uphill," she said.

They switched and she sat on his ankles this time.

It was harder, doing sit-ups uphill. Christopher put his hands at his side this time, instead of behind his back. She could see him cheating by gripping the grass.

Each time she counted a number she drew out the sound to make it harder on him.

At seven or eight, Martha shouted up to them to come down for chocolate milk.

Christopher pulled his ankles out from under Ursula and turned to bound down the slope, shouting "race you" over his shoulder.

"That's not fair," shouted Ursula, happy to be chasing after her brother who was not a brother.

Weeping Mountain

Ocho was adjusting to life without the rat's brain in his gut. He wondered whether this was how other people felt all the time, or whether this was something special. He wanted to ask someone about having a rat's brain in their gut. Someone who knew what he was going through.

He couldn't ask Ruth and he couldn't ask his parents because they were all dead.

There was nobody at work he could speak to. In the lift he stared sideways at a woman to see if he could tell whether she had a rat's brain in her gut. The woman closed her coat to cover the area Ocho was staring at. Ocho turned around and pretended to look in the lift mirror. The overhead lights showed up the pig hairs on his ears.

He asked his boss what his gut felt like. His boss was a jaded man who only wanted to avoid difficulty in his life. He patted his gut and said that bread made him bloated but he couldn't give it up.

Ocho thought about ringing Carthage and Clare, but he hadn't seen them in years. Not since Ruth died. He had met Clare in the butcher's shop around then. She had changed her hair. He asked her how things were and she usual-schmusualled him. Ocho had asked about Carthage and she said it was his birthday soon so she was buying meat for a birthday barbecue. She didn't invite Ocho or ask how he was, even though Ruth and his parents had died recently. At the time, Ocho was trying so hard to be nice around Clare that he didn't take offence, but when he thought about it afterwards it stung to think about how pointed her lack of interest was.

Ocho thought about when Ghost Mountain first appeared and how there were other mountains in the news about the same time that all turned out to be hoaxes. One of them was called Weeping Mountain because it would cry intermittently. People used to gather to watch it cry and project spiritual significance onto the fact that it cried. They thought of Weeping Mountain as living. As something with feelings. They thought that Weeping Mountain wept in despair at the world. It brought out their caring nature and made them want to make Weeping Mountain happy so that it wouldn't cry anymore. Even after people realised that Weeping Mountain was merely a seasonal phenomenon caused by changes in the water table under the limestone, there remained a small number of people whose fascination with the mountain was unchanged. For them, the symbolic weeping was no less significant for having a known cause.

At Weeping Mountain, the car park was a longish walk away. Why did they never build car parks near to mountains, Ocho wondered. Then he thought that maybe the car park was older than Weeping Mountain. That maybe Weeping Mountain had simply appeared, like Ghost Mountain had. Like Ruth believed Ghost Mountain had done. Ocho forgot that he believed differently.

It rained heavily along the wooded track to Weeping Mountain. Ocho walked by the verge to shelter under the overhanging branches. Every now and then the rain would collect into drops too heavy for a branch tip to hold and would fall down the nape of his neck. It seemed colder than the rain that fell on his face. As he walked, he saw frogs jump from the path into the pine needles off the track. He stopped to look at them. He had never seen real frogs before. They were yellow and smaller than he had expected.

As he walked, Ocho thought about how the rain would seep into the water table and make the mountain weep. He wanted to see that even if it wasn't real weeping.

Ocho arrived at the foot of Weeping Mountain. It had stopped raining and there was steam coming from the grass in a clearing. Some people in bright jackets descended from the slope and Ocho almost asked them whether they had seen the mountain weeping.

Ocho had been used to walking around Ghost Mountain and had forgotten that for most people the whole point of a mountain was to climb it. There were some muddy tracks up the side of Weeping Mountain where walkers had to step on protruding, slippery stones, but there was no circuit around it.

Ocho strained with the effort of the steep walk up the slope. He was wearing his boots, which he had never truly broken in, but they were not the hillwalking type. Whenever he lost grip, his legs stretched into splits, stabbing his groin with painful heat. He grabbed onto leafy branches or boulders to save himself from slipping. There was water running in the opposite direction. Was this thin ribbon of run-off considered weeping?

From the summit he could see that the rain had made the air all around him grey. The panorama was beautiful, but Ocho was not looking for beauty. He walked around on the rocky summit to see if he could find the weeping. The wind was blowing from all directions and the wetness under his jacket suddenly felt cold. He drank from his water bottle and ate into his peanut butter sandwich. He no longer added butter to the peanut butter even though this left the sandwich dry. There was a strange contrast in being so wet yet eating a dry sandwich. At least there were no wasps, he thought with a sort of relief. He listened out for the sound of weeping, but the wind was too violent against his hood and it was impossible to tell one thing from another. He stepped forward towards the edge of an outcrop, one leg behind the other for balance. As always in this type of situation there was a temptation to do something dangerous, but he quelled it. Peeking over the edge, he saw that water was gushing from the mountain. It had no single source. There was no obvious opening. It seemed to weep from the ground itself.

Ocho removed his hood. He felt the wind buffeting his face and swirling in his earholes and paining his front teeth and rushing through his wet hair and attacking the gaps in his clothing. He closed his eyes and thought about the mountain weeping. He thought about Ruth. He thought about his parents. He thought about how dead they were. He looked inside himself to where the rat's brain used to be in his gut but all he found was the sadness searching around his body, looking for the Ochos that used to be in there. The mountain wept out its water table but Ocho did no weeping.

He kicked his peanut butter crusts off the edge.

It was even trickier coming down Weeping Mountain than it was climbing it. Ocho cursed the mud and he cursed his boots and he cursed his waterproof coat for its shortcomings. With each slip, his clothes became more sodden and stained.

Ocho had begun to notice something. Though his curses were at their most authentic and creative, they rose within him only to subside back to wherever they had come from. Without the rat's brain, there was no traction. The curses sank unclaimed. This interested him.

At the foot of Weeping Mountain, there was a horseshoe of zipped-up tents around a dampened communal campfire. The grey light of the day was dimming as the rain continued to attack the mountain. The tents glowed from the inside.

Ocho was reminded of the cultish community that had taken Ruth from him. He hated these people by association. He hated them calmly but it was hate all the same.

Ocho ran around the back of the tents and lifted the pegs that held the guy ropes – he threw the pegs into the dense gorse and used the loose ropes to drag the tents down. He shouted loud indistinct noises, as if he were corralling horses. Alarm and confusion was aroused. He saw a man tangled within his collapsing tent. It would have been so easy to kick him in the head. One kick and it would have been all over for him.

Ocho ran in his heavy boots, back along the track he had come. He listened out for an angry mob in pursuit, but there was only the cacophony of the storm – the full trees had amplified the wind and made it sound worse than it was. There was now a murderous dark all around him as he trotted in his soaking clothes back to his car.

Ocho drove back to Ghost Mountain and the rotten banana house. He looked out for Ghost Mountain from the road but could tell it only as the darkest part of the dark. The house was locked, so he slipped around the back to try the kitchen door. He forced it open. Inside, he fell over some boxes that had been stacked there since his last visit. Too exhausted to think about it, he sank into the old chair in the kitchen and slept under many irrelevant dreams.

The next morning, he was woken by the sensation of being watched. Dust motes hung in the too-bright light. A young boy stood in front of him, barefoot and in pyjamas that were too small. He was holding a theodolite above his head.

The stillness between them added to the strangeness of the moment.

"What's your name?" asked Ocho.

"Are you my father?" asked the boy.

"I don't have any children. I'm not anybody's father," replied Ocho.

Ocho leaned forward to say something, but the boy stepped back reflexively and dropped the heavy theodolite, breaking Ocho's jaw and knocking him unconscious.

Is he dead?

Dominic had been in bed with Elaine when his phone rang. They had coupled early.

Dominic answered and walked around topless in his pyjama bottoms and scratched his pigeon chest as he listened.

Elaine could hear a woman speaking with urgency and worry.

So that's what she sounds like, Elaine thought. She is a voice. Elaine had imagined her as a body.

Dominic asked matter-of-factly, "Is he dead?" then walked into the bathroom and peed while still on the call.

There was a coarseness to Dominic that Elaine had never got used to.

He returned shortly afterwards and tossed his phone on the bed.

"I have to go over to Martha's house," he said. "She says there's a man on her floor, unconscious, with a theodolite."

He said this as though it was a normal combination of words.

Dominic pulled his jeans over the underwear he had worn in bed. Traces of Elaine were still on him. He went to the bathroom to brush his teeth, except the teeth he was missing.

Elaine sat up in the bed and listened to Dominic gargle. She thought about how even though young women were so pretty and older men were not so generally pretty, an older man with two missing teeth could still be a cause of jealousy.

"Don't get caught up in a murder scene," she said lightly, as Dominic leaned in for a goodbye kiss.

Elaine was reassured that he had not showered. That he would arrive at Martha's house with her smell still on him.

Ursula presented herself in the doorway and asked where Captain had gone.

Elaine explained.

Ursula looked disappointed to have slept through her chance to go to Christopher's house.

"Do you want to come into my bed so I can do your hair?" offered Elaine, but Ursula had already turned away.

Elaine heard Ursula say "Shit in a bag" to herself as she walked down the stairs.

Elaine lay down but she could no longer feel the warm pressure of Dominic on top of her. All she could feel was his absence.

She got out of bed and picked up the pyjama bottoms Dominic had abandoned. She put them on. His legs were so much longer than hers. Out of proportion to the difference in their heights, it seemed. She took off her top and stood as he had stood. Scratched her chest as he had scratched. His chest had steely grey hair. Hers was smooth except for some light down. His belly hung like a pouch whereas hers spilled over the waistband all around. Like risen dough. She pinched it. Hurt it.

What would she do in his position, she thought.

"Shit in a bag," she muttered.

Elaine changed back into her own pyjamas and followed Ursula downstairs.

In the living room, Ursula had taken down Elaine's portrait of Dominic from its easel. Her half-started/half-finished portrait. Ursula was using her own coloured pencils to finish the picture. Big angry lines that sank into the canvas. All his teeth blacked-out.

Elaine called out but Ursula would not be interrupted.

So Elaine took up a pencil and knelt down beside her so that they could ruin the portrait together.

Ruin Dominic before he could ruin them.

Food

Ocho woke, alive and sitting in the old kitchen chair.

The town drunk was bent over staring into his eyes. A woman was standing behind him, chewing her thumbnail.

"He's not dead anyway," said the town drunk.

Ocho tried to speak but immediately halted with a pain that was itself unspeakable. He pointed to his injured jaw as if to say he would not be trying to speak again.

The town drunk explained to the woman that he knew the man, though didn't know his name, and that the man had often stayed in the house when it was empty.

The misunderstanding untangled itself.

They discussed for a moment whether to call an ambulance, and quickly dismissed the possibility of either party calling the police on the other. The town drunk said that if the man was agreeable, he was welcome to rest up at his house where they could call a doctor.

Ocho was sore and concussed. The town drunk led him out through the front door of the rotten banana house to wherever they were going. The concussion had left Ocho feeling docile. His vision was blurry. His thoughts seemed to skitter away from him. Through the front window, he saw the boy sitting watching cartoons with the busted theodolite on his lap.

Ocho leaned over and vomited onto nearby nettles, before closing the gate behind him. The town drunk had told him his name, but no sooner had Ocho heard it than it slipped down the back of his brain and was lost.

They cut across the field to walk past Ghost Mountain. It stood in half-shade, half-light, manifestly itself. It was the first time Ocho had walked on Ghost Mountain since he had been to Weeping Mountain. Even with his soreness and concussion the clarity in his gut was still there.

The town drunk repeated that his name was Dominic. Ocho tried to make the name stick. Thought of all the Dominics he had known. He thought of a Dominican friary he had visited on a school tour. He tried to remember the flag for the Dominican Republic. And tried to remember whether it was a different country to Dominica.

He once again vomited on some nettles, leaving them steaming.

Dominic was talking about Ghost Mountain. About how he often walked around it with his family and his dog and how he often talked to Ghost Mountain whenever he walked there on his own. Said it was "deaf as a mountain" which made it a good listener.

He was speaking to Ocho as if he too were deaf as a mountain. So long as Ocho didn't speak Dominic treated him as a mountainous confidante.

Ocho's jaw throbbed and was swelling but was not as sore as he imagined a broken jaw would feel. There was a trauma memory of the sensation of the theodolite hitting him. His brain kept recreating the moment of impact. It had been a smooth action. His head had snapped to the side with no resistance.

Ocho's temporary muteness encouraged candour from Dominic. He expounded on the family history of a bunch of people Ocho had never heard of, only to realise he was talking about the woman in the rotten banana house, her son and her ex-husband. The husband had some connection to the theodolite that had broken Ocho's jaw. All Ocho wanted to do was sleep. He wanted to lie down on Ghost Mountain. Was it bad to sleep with a concussion? He had some idea that it was bad and that the Dominican Republic and Dominica were different countries and that one of them had a parrot on its flag.

Dominic walked on ahead as he spoke, pausing every now and then to let Ocho catch-up. When he turned to offer Ocho a tissue to press against his split lip, Ocho noticed that Dominic was missing his front teeth. Ocho ran his tongue around his own teeth to check whether he was missing any. His tongue was numb and swollen so it was hard to tell.

Dominic stopped to point out a bird carrying off a leveret. Said it was a buzzard. Perhaps the young hare was already dead before the bird found it.

"Everything is food," said Dominic. "As far as I can tell, that's the only point of life."

He looked directly at Ocho as if to see whether this moment of philosophy had registered on his swollen face.

"The whole reason you and I are on this earth," Dominic elaborated, "Is so wolves have something to eat."

Dominic set off again, his shoes squelching in the muddy track.

"Not too far to go," said Dominic. "You're doing great."

Ocho's boots had sunk into the mud and slurped as he lifted his feet.

Amid the fog of the concussion and his nausea and his swollen jaw, Ocho realised that his boots no longer pinched him. He wondered whether he had finally broken them in.

Recuperation

Ocho recuperated on Dominic's couch.

The doctor had been called to the house. He said Ocho's jaw was not broken as far as he could tell, but that it was badly bruised and swollen and maybe even dislocated. Ocho would need to go to the hospital, he said. As Ocho found it painful to speak, the doctor asked Dominic what had happened. Dominic, not wanting to incriminate Christopher, said a theodolite had fallen off a shelf and hit Ocho on the jaw. He and the doctor went back and forth about what a theodolite was. Dominic also explained how he had lost his front teeth. The doctor took out a false tooth of his own and showed it to Dominic.

After the doctor had left, Ocho could hear Dominic talking to his wife in the hall. His wife was called Elaine. They whispered loudly about whether it was a good or bad idea to get so involved. She said he should have asked her first. That he needed to think things through. Dominic defended his reasoning without resorting to criticising his wife. Ocho admired that. He heard Dominic explain about the theodolite. Every time Ocho heard the word "theodolite" he could feel the ghost of the theodolite's impact on his jaw.

Dominic brought him some soup. Ocho's mouth was still numb so he couldn't tell what flavour it was. He slurped the soup on the good side of his mouth. Whenever he drooled, Dominic leaned over and dabbed Ocho's chin with a tissue. A little girl watched them from the doorway. He recognised her from Ghost Mountain.

Ocho wondered whether Dominic's solicitude had something to do with dissuading him from pressing charges or suing. But Ocho was too drowsy from painkillers and too sore to sue anybody.

Dominic sat in the lounger opposite Ocho. The lounger was old and worn and stuck in a reclining position. Dominic said Ocho was welcome to stay for a few days. Dominic said he felt partly responsible, as he had brought the theodolite to the Ghost Mountain house. However, he said Ocho would have to stay somewhere else after he was better, as his wife was not especially keen on the arrangement.

"That's not what I said!" called Elaine from the other room.

Because Ocho couldn't speak, it gave licence to Dominic to talk without interruption, except when his wife called from the next room to correct his exaggerations. Dominic explained that his wife was a gifted artist and that she had painted the pictures that were on the walls around them. The paintings all looked the same to Ocho. Dominic said Elaine had painted his portrait too but that it had got damaged.

Ocho could see why Dominic would make a good study for a portrait. It was mesmerising to watch the gap in his teeth. But Ocho's eyes began to shutter as he listened to Dominic. He could hear Dominic's voice in his head. It was a dream voice where he could get a sense of its meaning from the tone and inflections, even though he was no longer picking out individual words. His head felt too heavy for his neck so he tipped it back and sailed off to sleep with his mouth open. If felt like a numb sleep. A painkiller sleep.

When he stirred, however long later, the little girl was sitting on a stool at his side and painting the nails on his left hand. She had painted them in little girl colours: cerise, lavender, puce. Ocho remembered Ruth's coral nail polish. That coral was a shade not a colour. Why had he said that? The little girl was a messy painter, not like her mother, who must have a steady hand. The nail polish went outside the lines of his nails. It didn't bother Ocho and he pretended to be asleep. In a way it was beautiful to him that he was having his nails painted while he slept and while his face was all swollen and sore. The girl was talking to him as he slept. Like he was her customer at a beauty salon. She asked him about his holidays and told him all about Crabs. He knew who Crabs was. He had seen him so often at Ghost Mountain and heard Dominic call his name. Where did the name come from, he wondered? He would ask Dominic that as soon as he could speak again.

Ocho broke wind as he pretended to sleep. The girl snickered. The painkillers that soothed his poor jaw were relaxing other muscles too. It gave Ocho no small pleasure to have made the girl laugh.

The tiredness that came over him was not an exhausted tiredness. It was not a worn-out tiredness. It was a tiredness that felt like a good place. His sailed off again and his dreams were full of colour.

Cerise, lavender, puce.

Wrestling

The next morning, Ocho lay on the couch where he had slept, and watched professional wrestling on the TV. He had eaten the porridge that was made for him. The little girl, who he learned was called Ursula, spied on him from the doorway, then shrank back whenever he turned to look at her. Ocho placed his hands outside his blanket so Ursula could see that he liked his new nails. On the TV, a bald wrestler hit a masked wrestler over the head with a chair. Ocho could feel the ghost of the theodolite impact as he saw the chair fall.

He had forgotten to take his painkillers and his jaw throbbed. His tongue felt spongy in his mouth.

Elaine came into the room to take his bowl away. He gave her a thumbs up. Ocho was still unable to speak clearly. Whenever he tried to say something it came out like a lowing sound. He had tried speaking when Elaine brought his porridge, but she couldn't understand him. He had to repeat the words several times, even though it hurt a lot. All he had meant to say was "never mind" but it ended up being a whole big deal.

Elaine handed him some clothes and a towel. She said he could have Dominic's old pyjamas but she had gone out and bought him some new underwear, as she wasn't sure what he had with him, probably nothing. She didn't know whether he planned to go to hospital for an x-ray or what. They'd have to find somewhere for him to stay, she said, now that Christopher and his mother had moved into the Ghost Mountain house. Dominic was trying to find him a job at the heel bar.

Ocho realised that they thought he was homeless now that the rotten banana house was taken. They didn't know he already had a job and a house.

He saw that Elaine had left nail polish remover on the coffee table.

Ocho showered. The warm water felt strange on his jaw. The mirror was steamed up but anyway, he had no interest in seeing what condition his face was in. Even the thought of it brought back the ghost of the theodolite impact on his jaw.

The girl's nail polish was pretty good. It didn't wash off in the shower or anything.

Ocho felt sleepy and clean after the shower.

The wrestling was over so he decided to nap on the couch.

Elaine asked if she could paint him.

He gave her a thumbs up again and saw that his painted nails caught her eye.

"Probably best that you've still got the nail polish," she said. "It will look good in the picture."

Elaine sat looking at him for a long time. So long that he almost forgot she was about to paint him. He wondered whether it was a form of artist's hypnosis. Getting him to relax so his pose wouldn't look too posed.

He became aware that his jaw was hanging slightly open and offset. When he tried to close it, the bite wouldn't quite fit back the way it used to.

His painkillers were starting to take effect. That, along with the afterglow of the shower, made him feel dreamy, though not yet sleepy. When he snapped out of it, Elaine was already painting.

Had Ocho felt normal and had his mouth been working he would have asked her about the portrait. He would have told her all about the rat's brain that used to be in his gut and asked whether she had one too. He would have asked whether artists knew about such things. What did it mean?

Ocho pondered these thoughts for some time before he realised that his eyes had closed and he was in a shallow painkiller sleep. His body and mind were conserving energy. It felt comfortable to close his eyes and let the thoughts play out on the inside of his eyelids.

His mouth felt warm and wet. It felt numb but it didn't feel like nothing. He could feel the breath from Elaine's nose on his cheek as she kissed him. She kissed him in a soft pecking way and then put her top and bottom lip around his top lip and sucked gently. Her tongue played too, acting like a lip. It might have lasted a few seconds or it might have been shorter than that. Ocho was lucid enough to realise his role was to play at being asleep, whether he was or not.

But something tempted him to open his eyes. Maybe he wanted to be sure that he definitely wasn't asleep, or maybe he wanted to be part of what was happening. He opened one eye for one moment. It was a compromise he allowed himself.

As he opened that eye, he saw that Elaine was indeed leaning over him and kissing him gently and furtively. Perhaps gentle because furtive. Her eyes were closed.

And then he saw that Ursula was watching them from the doorway. She drew back when her gaze locked with Ocho's open eye.

Likeness

Elaine was working on the likeness in the Ocho portrait. The kiss had been spontaneous or maybe it was anything but spontaneous. Maybe it was the culmination of all her doubts about herself, about Dominic, and about Dominic and Martha. Perhaps it was an inevitable kiss. Ocho was only the second person she had ever kissed. In a way, she preferred the Ocho kiss to the kisses she had had with Dominic. With Dominic it was a sloppy wrestling of tongues. She always had to pause periodically to catch her breath or wipe her chin. She could never visualise what was going on in her mouth when it was happening. With the Ocho kiss, however, she was the kisser and he was the kissed. She realised she preferred that. It was calmer and she was able to express the kiss better. During the kiss, she did not feel passion and she did not feel any love-like emotion. It was not a crush and it was not an arousal. It wasn't even a curiosity about the types of kisses that were out there in the world.

She kissed him because of creative rain.

As she was painting Ocho, the creative rain came on very strongly. It was overwhelming and rushed through her like rapids. She kissed him to dissipate the creative rain. There was never a need to examine the why and the how that lay behind what triggered creative rain and its intensity. Creative rain washed away those questions just like it washed away everything else. That was where the clarity of creative rain came from.

Ocho's face was swollen and yellowing with bruises. It changed every day. Elaine wanted to capture him as he was at the time of the kiss. By the afternoon, his face would already have changed. For the first time, Elaine began to understand likeness in her painting. It was not about recording what somebody looked like so that they could always look that way. It was about capturing a moment of change. A simultaneous moment of change in the subject and in the artist. Ocho's swollen face was changing as his body healed itself, a process that the body knew without ever learning or being shown how. And Elaine was changing after kissing only the second person in her life. She was changed because she had always thought kissing was something other people understood better than she did. Now she realised that she understood it just as well. Her body knew all about kissing without ever learning or being shown how.

The portrait said all this without speaking for her or speaking for Ocho. By comparison or by contrast, the painting of Dominic was purely descriptive. It was like an entry in the birth register.

The painting of Ocho was different.

The painting of Ocho was like a kiss.

Rocks

Ocho lay awake on the couch, his blanket half kicked off. The dark was all around him. His eyes adjusted to it. His brain was numb and sleepless from the painkillers. He was awake enough to have thoughts but not so awake he could think them through or think them away.

Even though his rat's brain was gone, things were still happening. *He* was still happening. It was undeniable. It was impossible for him to remain a neutral force in the world. Every day that he lived, he was accumulating more past. Everything he did was a cause that would have some effect. It was impossible not to be a cause. Even when he lay asleep and immobile, the universe kissed him. And the universe provided a witness for the kiss. Now three people had more past. And more causes. That's how things went.

Ocho rose to see whether the painkiller constipation had loosened.

He dressed himself in case Elaine saw him. In case Ursula saw him. In case the universe saw him and made more causes. More past.

Ocho put on his sweater. And then he slipped into his boots. His boots that had been finally broken in.

He let himself out of the house.

He wanted to walk to Ghost Mountain. Ghost Mountain, which, alone, caused things but was never affected by them.

The moon was bright with blurred edges. Silhouetted clouds floated past it. Its light came and went.

Ghost Mountain was all colourless light and dark. Like an old movie.

Ocho thought about Ruth and how she was scattered there. But Ghost Mountain seemed to have absorbed everything. He couldn't feel anything of Ruth there.

How strange that he had found himself there so often.

What was Ghost Mountain to him?

It wasn't a challenge.

It wasn't an obstacle.

It wasn't his enemy and it wasn't his friend.

It didn't matter and it didn't not matter.

Ocho's jaw felt the cold. He thought this was a good thing. That the feeling was coming back.

He attempted to say something.

"Ocho, Ocho," he called.

He drooled a little and his jaw didn't set right after he said it. But the sound was clear and it didn't hurt too much to speak.

He began climbing Ghost Mountain's leeward side.

The moon cast his shadow before him, making him look longer than he was. His shadow led him up there.

"Ocho, Ocho," he sang quietly to himself, like a bird. Like a drooling bird.

Ocho decided he would stop paying his mortgage. His half mortgage. Just like his parents had stopped paying their two half mortgages. He didn't want his widower house anymore.

He would leave his job, if he hadn't already lost it.

He would lie there on Ghost Mountain. On its cold, bald summit.

The buzzards would take him away, just like they had done with the leverets.

Ruth was dead.

His parents were dead.

The rat's brain was dead.

His jaw hurt and he possibly had a concussion.

He didn't want to accumulate any more past.

He didn't want to be a cause anymore.

Ocho approached the summit and climbed the last few steps on all fours, like how he used to climb the stairs in his house. He looked out over the landscape. From the ground every inch of the world had a separate name, yet from a height it looked indivisible. But there was not one thing he could see that he could connect to. Not even the mountain beneath his feet. Not even the body he looked out from.

He turned around to see where the rotten banana house was. There was one yellow rectangle burning even though it was later than late.

He was drooling but couldn't purse his lips enough to spit.

Had he been on a cliff he could have thrown himself off. But it was a small mountain, with sides barely steep enough to roll down.

Ocho began collecting rocks. Flat and heavy rocks mostly. He piled them in one heap, shuttling back and forth as he collected more. Some of the rocks he wanted were embedded in the mud and couldn't be shifted. He began to tire. He was sweating heavily but the cold air chilled the sweat as it broke.

Ocho lay down among the rocks. He began covering himself, starting with his feet. The rocks kept slipping from his shins. He worried he wouldn't have enough rocks. He covered himself up to his waist. He tried moving his legs, but they were pinned and he was now too tired to undo what he had started.

Rock by rock he covered his middle until he needed to lie down and reach out to the side to cover his chest. His tailbone was resting on a protruding rock. He regretted not checking more thoroughly the ground he had chosen to lie on.

Ocho tried to lift himself up. Though he was certainly pinned, he could manage to move enough for some of the rocks to slide off to the side. There were not enough rocks piled onto him. He would still be able to rescue himself if he wanted to. He was unable to lift heavy rocks one-handed, and so his arms could only add rocks that would be light enough to remove if necessary. His body would always be capable of saving itself.

Ocho felt around for a heavy rock to his left. It was poor planning not to have left it above his head where he could have reached it with two hands. Reached and lifted it above his face where he could have let it drop. Drop onto his jaw with the weight of a hundred theodolites.

He moved rocks to pin his right side, but his left arm remained mostly free.

The weight on his chest made him wheezy. He again tested his legs and his hips. He was pinned but not crushed. His free hand reached around but there were no rocks close enough for him to add to the pile.

The protruding rock continued to trouble his tailbone.

Cold drops of rain began to tickle the right side of his face, where his free hand couldn't reach. He winked and squinted to relieve the sensation. Blew upwards from the right side of his mouth. His swollen mouth that had been kissed.

This reminded him of Ursula.

The cold, the tiredness, the dizziness, the half-success/half-failure of the venture, all pinned him there as much as the rocks did.

He could breathe but his breaths were short and inadequate.

A tidal drowsiness began to sap him. He leaned to the side and vomited. The potent hot drool ran down his right cheek and into his ear.

In his mind he had had a picture of his end as something still and heavy. Like the rocks. Like Ghost Mountain itself. But if the end was to be a struggling form of failure, then let it be that, he thought.

He tried to conjure the thought that he might be lying there with Ruth and his parents. But he could not feel their warmth. He could not remember their warmth. Just like he could no longer remember their voices.

Ocho thought about all the people who had died in their sleep and who had been thought to have died a good death. But some people who died in their sleep must have died among nightmares. When Ocho's lids closed, he saw the nightmare of what he had forgotten to say to Ursula. He had wanted to explain that her mother had only kissed him to suck the poison from his lips and make him better. He had meant to say that to Ursula, or leave her a note, or use some other method he had not fully thought through, but he had forgotten and now it was too late to lie to protect her. Now it lay at the back of his mind with all the other unfinished thoughts of his life.

More past.

More causes.

Ocho was blinking and awake and exhausted when Christopher discovered him there the next morning.

Christopher looked down at Ocho.

Ocho looked up at Christopher.

Ocho could see that it was bright and already a new day, and that he had not died in the night, though he had experienced many deaths during that time.

Christopher was calm and unspeaking. He was wearing a jacket with the zip open. He disappeared off for a few moments.

As Ocho lay there, he didn't know whether he felt disappointed. Given the choice, he didn't know whether he would have preferred to have died in the night or to be freed and continue living with more past and more causes.

Christopher returned, carrying rocks. Flat, heavy rocks. The heaviest he could carry, though not as heavy as those Ocho, even in his weakened state, had been able to assemble.

There, Christopher calmly laid the other rocks onto Ocho. Onto his free arm first and then under his chin. Christopher carefully placed more rocks onto Ocho's body, adding further layers to Ocho's work from the night.

Finally, only Ocho's face was uncovered.

Christopher knelt above him, looking down.

It was as if Christopher was waiting for a signal.

Ocho lay there passively. Concentrating hard not to communicate anything. Concentrating hard not to create a cause.

As Christopher lifted the largest stone he could manage above Ocho's face, Ocho braced himself for the ghost of the theodolite impact on his jaw.

But instead, Christopher rested the rock gently onto Ocho's face, flattening his nose and closing off one nostril.

To that rock he added another, and then more.

Whenever a rock slid off to the side, Christopher replaced it, patted it down and wedged smaller rocks to keep the structure stable.

Christopher was so careful in his work.

Christopher didn't hurt Ocho at all.

When Christopher was done, Ocho could hear the zip of his jacket jingle off into the distance.

Ocho felt heavy and numb. He could no longer feel the protruding rock on his tailbone. It felt like his inhalation only reached the roof of his mouth before he had to exhale it again. Like he was only taking in his own warm, moist breath. Like he was swilling the same mouthful of air over and over.

It was a few days before Ocho was found.

It was his left hand that was discovered. His left hand with the nail polish on it.

It was the only part of him that was visible from under the rock pile.

Maybe he had worked it free, or perhaps the rock that was covering it had simply slid off in the rain.

It was Dominic who noticed, when he chased up Ghost Mountain after Crabs and found the dog licking Ocho's hand.

Police

The police called over to speak to Dominic. They said it was just an informal chat and not an interview as such.

Even though the informal chat was about him finding yet another dead body, and despite their uneasiness at the sinister association with Ghost Mountain, they were glad to see him. It had been a while.

"The man who fixes our windows sends his regards," the sergeant said.

Dominic had made them tea.

Apart from the sergeant the two other police officers were new and must have joined since Dominic had last been at the station. Nevertheless, they knew of him and were glad to finally meet the man they had heard so much about.

Ursula was playing quietly at the window with Dominic's two front teeth. It was a game where the teeth were supposed to be horses or some other jumping animal and she was voicing their adventures.

"So, tell us again how you found the man," requested the sergeant. He and his two colleagues held notebooks and small pencils.

"It was Crabs who found him," said Dominic. "Crabs! Crabs!"

Crabs came in and started licking Dominic's hand. The police officers noted that the dog was called Crabs.

"It's OK – we don't interview dogs," said the sergeant.

The other two officers crossed out their note about Crabs.

Dominic explained that he had followed Crabs up Ghost Mountain and that when he saw the man's hand protruding, he lifted the rocks from him, but it was too late.

"What time was that?" asked an officer who was not the sergeant.

"He meant it was too late – the man was already dead," said the sergeant. "What time was it though?" he asked Dominic. As he was the sergeant, he had first dibs on all the right questions.

Dominic explained that it was the morning time – before breakfast. Crabs always woke with a full bladder in the mornings and needed to be brought out first thing. Crabs liked licking salty things so drank a lot.

"It's a shame that you moved the stones, though," said the sergeant. "They're sort of our only evidence."

"Evidence of what?" asked Dominic.

The sergeant looked at his two colleagues.

"A crime," he said calmly, after a few heavy moments of silence.

Dominic rubbed his chin.

"I hadn't thought about it that way," he said. "But if I hadn't moved the stones, and he had been alive, and he then died, wouldn't that have been a crime? Manslaughter maybe?"

The two officers didn't write down Dominic's question. They had a police instinct for when a note would be unhelpful.

"That's a counterfactual," said the sergeant. "Counterfactuals are of no interest in matters of the law. Otherwise, murderers could claim that their victims would have gone on to become serial killers in the future and so their murder was justified. Where would that leave us?"

Dominic, who had respect for the law, also had respect for this viewpoint.

"So, what's your theory?" asked Dominic.

The sergeant paused a moment and then signalled to the officers to put down their pencils.

"If it was a murder, we don't understand why the murderer would go to so much trouble to make such a conspicuous and labour-intensive grave," said the sergeant.

"Though he did have unexplained injuries," added one of the officers.

The sergeant turned, displeased by the interruption.

"I meant on his jaw," said the officer apologetically to the sergeant.

"Oh, that," said Dominic. "That's from an unrelated theodolite injury. He spent a few days with us to recover from it."

"Keep that to yourself for now," said one of the officers who wasn't the sergeant. He blushed when he realised everyone was looking at him, even Ursula.

"We know that it can't have been suicide," continued the sergeant in a lowered voice, conscious of Ursula's presence. "We tried it up there with him" – he pointed with his thumb to his blushing colleague. "It's impossible to cover oneself. Even if it were technically possible, you always leave enough of an escape route. It's instinct."

Dominic looked at the officer. There was indeed rock dust on his uniform from when he had been nearly buried alive in the line of duty.

Dominic poured them more tea.

"We need a photo for the newspaper, so we can find any witnesses. I don't suppose you have one from when he stayed here?"

Dominic left the room and returned with Elaine's portrait.

The sergeant held it at arm's length.

"Who painted this?" asked the sergeant.

"My wife," said Dominic. "She's an artist."

"I thought it was by an artist, alright," said the sergeant. "Looks nothing like him." Catching himself, he added: "No offence."

"Likeness isn't as important as people think it is," said Dominic. "We don't know what the Mona Lisa really looked like."

The sergeant handed the painting back. "Not my area of expertise," he said.

In the local newspaper, the story said that Ocho had tried to build a tower of stones as a monument to his wife who had died on Ghost Mountain years ago, and that it had toppled over and crushed him. Anyone who had information on the accident was asked to get in touch.

The local newspaper also ran a story about Dominic and showed a picture of him with his teeth missing. In it he was holding Elaine's damaged portrait of him. They said he no longer drank or threw bricks, and that he was now married with a child and had found two dead bodies since he was last in the newspaper.

The piece about Dominic was hugely popular. One woman had a letter published in which she said that the painting of him was not a good likeness.

Nobody came forward about Ocho's death.

Memorial Service

Dominic and Elaine organised a memorial service for Ocho at the top of Ghost Mountain, where they would spread his ashes.

The stones that had buried him were still heaped in the general area where he had died.

Dominic had suggested that they organise a few stones into a cross shape to mark the spot. Elaine said this would be disrespectful as Ocho's wife had been a Satanist and perhaps Ocho was one too.

In addition to Dominic and Elaine and Ursula, Christopher attended with his mother.

It was the first time that Elaine had seen Martha in person.

Elaine's hair was short and androgynous. She wore no make-up or perfume. As usual, she had on a check shirt, jeans, walking boots and a waterproof windcheater.

Martha had corkscrew curls that flickered around her face. She wore a chunky green cardigan over a lemon-yellow dress. Her nail polish was chipped. Her hands gesticulated when she spoke and her face stretched and brightened in response to what other people said. To what Dominic said. Elaine thought she was very beautiful. She was differently beautiful to what Elaine had expected. There was a quiet wildness about her. Elaine could see that if Martha was in a room, the room would have a crush on her. That maybe even a mountain could have a crush on her. That Martha was a natural crush object and that a person could crush on her without wanting or meaning to. It could be completely impersonal. This made Elaine feel better about Dominic and Martha.

A middle-aged man they didn't recognise had joined them. He wore a suit but no coat. He shivered. Elaine heard him say to Dominic that he was Ocho's manager at work and that he had seen the details of the service in the local newspaper. He wanted to pay his respects. He said he didn't know Ocho well.

Ursula stood beside Christopher. She held Crabs back by his collar. They had forgotten to bring his leash. Crabs was licking Christopher's hand.

Dominic said a few words. It was windy so he had to shout a little. He spoke about Ocho and what little they knew of him. That he seemed a lonely man. That he was now being reunited with his wife, the Satanist. That his ashes would be scattered on the mountain he probably loved, or where he spent his time anyway. Dominic tried to make a point about how matter or energy couldn't be created or destroyed, but he rambled a little. He wasn't sure whether dead people were simply matter or had some energy too. In the end he said that people could look it up if they needed more detail.

He had made a flag, which he attached to the blackthorn branch he had been using as a walking stick lately.

He stabbed it into the ground and scattered Ocho's ashes around it.

Everyone stood silently for a minute, their heads bowed, their hands joined and hanging low in front of their privates.

The wind blew the flag off the stick and it tumbled down the side of Ghost Mountain.

"Leave it," said Dominic softly, as Ocho's manager moved to retrieve it.

Then Crabs broke free from Ursula and ran after the flag. Ursula chased after Crabs and Christopher chased after Ursula, overtaking her as they bounded down the windward side of the mountain.

Elaine stood staring at the quiet wildness of differently beautiful Martha, who was staring at Dominic, who was staring in the direction the children had gone.

Ghost Mountain

There was a storm that evening. It was loud and disorganised. On Ghost Mountain, whatever the storm had disturbed started the next day in its new place.

Afterwards, as before, Ghost Mountain was Ghost Mountain.

BOOK 3

Ursula

Ursula shared a house with three other people. She was twenty-five and had long ago woken up from her childhood.

In the house Ursula shared, she never knew what was really happening. It was a house with no hierarchy. Where nobody told anyone else what to do. Any housemates who needed to tell people what to do, or who liked to be told what to do, soon left. They were always unhappy when they left because they felt defeated without knowing by whom and by what. Ursula had gone through many housemates. Ursula had reached the point where she no longer saw housemates as friends or future friends. She didn't invest in them. She had lost interest in explaining to new people about her family or where she was from. She had become bored by her own biography. It didn't amount to anything more than the same kinds of facts that applied to everyone. A few things that had happened a long time ago.

Ursula didn't drink alcohol so she tended to get up earlier than everyone else. She liked to draw or paint before breakfast. She preferred to work with whatever energy she awoke with. Whatever energy was left over after the night. It was not energy from food and it was not energy from stimulation. It was the type of unattributable energy that was good for making pictures.

Her housemate's boyfriend had also got up early that morning. He came into the living room wearing running gear and was stretching at the chimney breast.

Ursula was sketching something, not him.

"What are you drawing?" he asked.

The boyfriend didn't understand that Ursula was in a state of mind.

Ursula didn't look up or answer.

As the boyfriend stretched, Ursula noticed that his calves were bald.

"Is this one of yours?" he asked about the painting above his head.

"It's the house's," said Ursula eventually and concisely.

"What's it supposed to be?"

"Barcelona," she said, still sketching.

The boyfriend looked at the painting. "But it's just loads of orange and yellow."

"That's what Barcelona looks like."

"Not when I was there," said the boyfriend.

Ursula hated boyfriend bullshit. Why was she even talking to this person?

"Your legs are pretty skinny for a runner," she said, still without looking up.

Ursula regretted saying this. Not because it was rude but because boyfriends liked attention. He would think it meant he was of interest.

The boyfriend left on his run but Ursula's sketching energy was already spoiled. Now her head was full of words. Her personality had woken up and chased away her picture.

Ursula went to check on her boyfriend, who was sleeping shirtless on his stomach in her bed. The covers were around his waist. The light picked out the down in the hollow of his back.

She never liked calling him her boyfriend. They socialised together and stayed in each other's beds, but she had no plans for him.

He looked nice on his stomach. It was a shame that her housemate's runner boyfriend with skinny bald calves had turned her off boyfriends that morning. Otherwise she might have lain down on her boyfriend's back.

"You have to get up. I have drawing stuff to do today," she said from the door.

She returned to the front room and started drawing her other hand for practice. Bullshit practice instead of the real drawing she had got up to do.

Ursula interrupted the drawing of her bullshit hand to look up pictures of Barcelona on her phone. She had never been there and wanted to see what colour it was.

Meat Gallery

U rsula had told her boyfriend that she had to do drawing that day. She had actually said "drawing stuff" which encompassed many things.

She went to a gallery that housed contemporary art but was in an old building. It had parquet floors and white walls and just the right amount of natural light. It had a little too much signage and the toilets were too far away and you couldn't bring in your backpack. Ursula had been in many galleries and they all more or less ran on the same setup.

She wanted to see the exhibition that had opened that weekend.

The pictures involved pieces of meat that had been nailed to wooden boards. Everything had meat in it. There was also some viscera and cartilage and sinews and ligaments and other connecting tissues.

Ursula didn't know whether it was all real meat or some other synthetic special effects material made to look like meat. If it was real meat, then how did they stop it going rancid? How did they stop smells? Did they use embalming fluid maybe?

Her thoughts on the process disturbed her thoughts on the pictures.

She liked to stand and look with her eyes out of focus. She wanted her mind to go out of focus too, not just her eyes. So that she wasn't thinking any words about the painting. Until her mind no longer said good or bad things about it. Until she became interested in the painting without becoming interested in her thoughts about the painting.

She stood in front of a large crucifixion, a meat crucifixion.

There was blood on the meat, which dripped steadily onto the parquet.

This concerned Ursula at first but then she doubted herself and thought that her concern was probably part of the intended effect. Ursula didn't liked paintings that tried to manipulate her.

She stood there and watched the meat and the blood. She worked hard to resist whatever message the artist was trying to convey. She wanted to withstand the manipulation. To withstand what the artist had tried to put in the painting.

"The blood's supposed to do that," interrupted the security guard.

The meat hung there. Ursula's attention hung there.

"I know," said Ursula, without taking her eyes off the picture.

After he had gone, she started to resent him for spoiling the whole point of the picture.

Why did security guards have to interfere?

Why did artists have to interfere?

Had she wanted to, it would have been possible to reach over and tear the meat from the picture and throw it against some other picture or throw it at the security guard.

All her life, Ursula had vertiginous flashes like this. Impulsive prompting to do something bad just to see what would happen. It scared her. She wasn't sure if she could rely on her resistance.

After the exhibition she ate ginger biscuits and had a mug of coffee in the gallery café.

She thought about the artist thinking about his meat pictures. How was he so sure they weren't terrible? That they weren't terrible art.

Ursula dipped a biscuit into her coffee. Loose crumbs floated like a constellation. She used her spoon to drink them like soup.

Ursula was fascinated at how she could spend a couple of hours pondering meat and then eat ginger biscuits without thinking of meat at all, even while the effect of pondering meat had not yet faded from her mind.

It fascinated her that she could hold such different images, such different processes, in her brain simultaneously.

And it fascinated her that during that whole time she had not thought about Christopher and yet had never for one moment truly forgotten him.

Christopher

As children, Ursula and Christopher had something that was different to friendship. It was an understanding. They were both missing something in their lives. Each became a wedge in the life of the other – something to fill and stabilise the gap, without closing it. Something to hold the gap open. Hold it open for the return of what was meant to fill it.

Christopher's childhood was sad in an ordinary way. When he was twelve, and without telling his mother, Christopher arrived at the house of his father, the former Clerk of Maps. At that time, his father had a new girlfriend who had two young children who looked like her. Christopher sat squashed between his father's girlfriend's children on the couch and watched television. His father's new girlfriend gave him popcorn and a carton of juice. His father asked him some questions from his armchair. He asked about school and about his mother. Whereas Christopher was pale and had untameable corkscrew hair, like his mother's, Christopher's father was lean and sallow, and wore a uniform from the crosstown train company. He was not much taller than Christopher himself.

He left Christopher sitting on the couch with the other children where they continued watching television. They watched a family game show and then a confusing programme for younger children. Christopher cried quietly to himself on the couch. The other children noticed and talked to each other about why Christopher was crying.

Christopher's father left for work without saying goodbye. Later, his father's girlfriend called the other children for dinner.

She didn't call Christopher for his dinner. She left him on the couch, hungry. It had been a long time since Christopher's father had left for work. Christopher didn't know how long as there was no clock on the wall, just a barometer.

While the others were eating, Christopher left without telling anyone and walked all the way home alone, where he got in trouble for causing worry.

Christopher had told all this to Ursula a few weeks afterwards while she leaned on his ankles so he could do sit-ups.

When it came to the final school summer before college, it had come up that neither of them had ever slept with anybody. Some kids in school had done it, or at least the girls who now had babies had done it. Neither Christopher nor Ursula had done it. They had agreed that if they were ever asked and had to answer, they could say they had done it with each other. Nobody would know that they hadn't. Or wouldn't.

Christopher had always been a beefy child but he had stopped growing in secondary school and Ursula had since overtaken him. He tended to let his corkscrew hair grow too long and then have it cut very short, so his hairstyle depended on where he was at in the growth cycle. His cheeks were flushed and his body had never lost its baby softness. Sometimes Ursula's friends laughed about him. Christopher still lived at the Ghost Mountain house, which added to the aura of unreality that surrounded him.

One morning, Christopher's father called to the house at Ghost Mountain. Christopher's parents had never got properly divorced and his father now wanted to marry his girlfriend. Christopher's mother had been difficult about this.

Finding the front door locked and unanswered, Christopher's father had entered through the back door. Moving through the house, he discovered the bedroom door wide open with Christopher sharing a double bed with his mother, he facing one wall and she the other. Christopher's father left quietly, without waking them.

Afterwards, he used this fact to press home the divorce.

Though Christopher's father swore that he never told anybody, it soon became famous around the school that Christopher slept with his mother.

It was all anyone at school talked about.

Ursula wanted to say that she sometimes crept into her mother's bed in the mornings, when her father was walking the dog. But she understood that everyone at school knew of her connection with Christopher, and that any effort to defend him would only condemn herself without saving him.

Ursula and Christopher separated into different worlds though remained on each other's periphery. Each was like a spider on the other's bedroom ceiling. They were never truly at ease without knowing where the other was and where they stood with each other. It was a form of external awareness. It was an energy field that extended beyond their bodies as far as the other person. It was sensitive to the slightest of disturbances.

After she left school, Ursula went to college and studied art, where she resented and had contempt for every piece of creative advice she was given. As soon as she graduated, she made it her vocation to paint and immerse herself in art until she had washed off everything she had been taught.

Christopher did not go to college. He and his mother moved out of the Ghost Mountain house and he left school before the final exams, to work on a farm, a pig farm. The farmer gave him money to buy feed. Christopher kept the money and instead charged the restaurants in town to take away their food waste, which he then fed to the pigs. After a while, he started taking away the restaurants' other waste and charging them for that too. He rented a van and would drive around at night and dump the waste in ditches or on the remote roadsides. Anywhere except Ghost Mountain.

Within a year or two he had enough money to do it legitimately and took a loan to buy an exhausted quarry. He charged the local authorities to put waste there, waste that he was also paid to collect.

In that way Christopher became successful and earned more money than any of the other people he had gone to school with. But to his classmates, he was not successful. He was considered a short pervert who worked with pigs and garbage.

Ursula had not spoken to him since the controversy about sleeping with his mother.

Ursula had not contacted Christopher.

Christopher had not contacted Ursula.

But the field of awareness between them remained, so much so that Ursula could not even look at a constellation of biscuit crumbs in her coffee without thinking about Christopher.

Elaine and Dominic

Elaine and Dominic remained married for the rest of their fifties, through their sixties and now deep into their seventies. They went to bed at different times, though always in the same day they awoke. Before midnight, in other words.

They slept in separate rooms. Dominic slept in a double bed and Elaine in a single bed, as she had done in the many years before they met.

It had been a long time since Dominic had come to her during the night.

They lived a life of peaceful companionship that was as close to love as made no difference.

They rose at different times, though both woke early – a habit from a life of dog walking. After Crabs died of cancer, Elaine said she couldn't stand to lose any more dogs and so they didn't get another. Even if Elaine had not said that she couldn't lose another dog, Dominic would not have suggested replacing Crabs. She loved him for that.

They ate dinner together in the evenings.

When it was Dominic's turn to cook, he prepared complicated meals that took too long and where some elements of the dish were ready before others, never a full plate ready at once.

Elaine had learned a small number of dishes that she could do well and had not learned any new recipes in many, many years.

They each accepted the other's cooking just as they accepted everything else about each other.

They showed a level of acceptance that was as close to love as made no difference.

They never criticised each other.

When Elaine left the bread lying out on the bread board, Dominic wrapped it up in a tea towel to keep it fresh.

Whenever Dominic spat in the sink without rinsing afterwards, Elaine would run her fingertips around and swish the water until the sticky phlegm whirled down the plughole.

Elaine sometimes charged her phone using Dominic's charger and he sometimes accidentally sent an email from her account whenever she had used his computer last and forgotten to log out.

Elaine cut Dominic's hornlike toenails for him and he tweezed her chin hairs for her.

They hardly spoke to one another because there was no unease that needed removing between them. Their routines had become so refined and simplified and familiar that they had evolved beyond the point of unintended meanings or misunderstandings.

Whatever physical needs they had, they took care of separately for themselves.

Over the years, Dominic had continued to have crushes. His crush objects changed from time to time and he was bad at hiding them. But Elaine had come to view a crush as its own punishment. The pining and displacement that a crush caused should have taught Dominic a lesson, but he was a man who had made a habit of pursuing things outside of himself, and when he moved on from drinking all those years ago, that pursuit became crushes.

Dominic had never been unfaithful in the physical sense, though his fantasies were often unfaithful.

Elaine, who had once killed a man who was not her husband, by kissing him in his sleep, forgave Dominic these venial transgressions of the imagination.

Unlike Dominic, Elaine felt no desire when she lay alone at night. Even this far into her long life, she still wondered whether this was normal and whether, by extension, she was normal.

For many Christmas gifts, Dominic had bought her paintings, paintings he had seen displayed on the railings in town. They were inferior to the pictures that Elaine would have been capable of painting, had she not given up all those years ago. After a time, she asked him to stop buying the awful railing paintings.

Every Christmas she bought him a razor and some aftershave.

Elaine did not like him growing a beard and though she accepted the beard as much as she accepted the man who wore it, her choice of present was a deliberate one.

Dominic used the razor to shave the nape of his neck and scented his beard with the aftershave before dinner in the evenings.

They accepted that one would die before the other at some stage, and in whatever order nature ordained. That would entail loss and absence, neither of which they could truly prepare for.

They also considered that one might decline before the other, and that the process of decline could be worse than dying. Like dying in slow motion, they guessed.

This too was something they could not prepare for.

If, after dinner, Elaine said that her eyes were getting weaker and that she could hardly read the newspaper, Dominic would say, "Let me be your eyes," and he would read the article for her, though a little too theatrically, for which she would correct, though not criticise, him.

If he was uncomfortably long passing a stool, Elaine would bring him a large glass of water to drink and refill it as often as necessary until he found relief.

Though they no longer shared carnal intimacy, they were comfortable with each other's bodies. It was not uncommon for one to be at the sink, brushing teeth, while the other chatted from the shower next to them.

Their lives meshed like sun-and-planet gears. There was a perfection to the way they lived a life that was truly theirs.

But it was only when Ursula visited that they noticed that their perfect harmony had been missing something.

Ursula Visiting

After the gallery, Ursula visited the house she continued to refer to as home.

Her thoughts about meat had not receded from her mind.

On the way there, she passed a man walking a dog and this reminded her of Crabs, who loved meat so much, and who once got tapeworm from eating raw meat.

But she disliked how the gallery art was trying to prompt her to think of everything as meat.

When she kissed Elaine on the cheek, though, she did think about how fleshy the lips were or how soft and responsive the cheek was and how she kissed with the same mouth she ate with.

The thought had already faded by the time she kissed Dominic. She had grown out of calling him Captain long ago.

Ursula told Elaine about the meat pictures.

Though Elaine no longer painted, she was still interested in the art world and Ursula's position in it. She had told Ursula all about creative rain, though Ursula had not experienced it herself. Ursula was jealous at first, but soon came to realise that her own creativity spoke a different language, that was all.

Ursula took out her phone and showed Elaine a picture from the gallery.

"I'd need to see it in person," said Elaine. "In the flesh, so to speak. There's no feedback from photos. The energy of it will be held in the paint."

Ursula looked at the picture on her phone.

"I can feel a sort of energy from the image, but maybe I'm recalling the energy I felt when I saw it at the gallery."

Ursula made a salad with no meat in it. She included hazelnuts, salty cheese and oranges. She made some for Elaine, knowing that Elaine needed a break from Dominic's food.

Because Elaine was an artist herself, she knew not to ask Ursula what she was working on or whether she was working on anything. She knew that paintings did not obey the rules of productivity, and in fact actively resisted them.

Elaine had also abided by her longstanding vow not to bring any family bullshit into their conversations. She didn't urge Ursula to pull her life together or earn more money or save more money or acquire property or make friends or spend her life more wisely.

For her part, Ursula did not patronise her mother.

"I think I'm going to paint Ghost Mountain," said Ursula. "Maybe a whole series. Maybe paint it and paint it for the rest of my life and then after I die it will become what I'm known for."

It was a statement rather than a suggested topic for conversation. Elaine understood this. It was good having an artist for a mother as Elaine never told Ursula what to paint or what not to paint. Elaine understood where pictures came from and that they did not come from the dinner table.

"Has anyone else painted it, apart from you?" asked Ursula.

"I didn't really paint it. I only used it as a background in a few pictures," said Elaine. "It never spoke to me that way."

Ursula thought about whether Ghost Mountain had ever spoken to her.

"Maybe I'll spend some time there and see if it speaks to me," said Ursula. "See what happens."

But Ursula knew that this conversation with Elaine was cover.

That in Ursula's mind, Ghost Mountain was code for Christopher.

That whenever she needed to talk about Christopher or find relief from the Christopher that was building up inside her, she would talk about Ghost Mountain. Even saying the words "Ghost Mountain" gave her peace, despite the concentrated effort it took to say them. An effort so intense that she almost stammered.

Ghost Mountain

The wind at Ghost Mountain was coming from all directions and shaped itself around its bulk. Clouds lay low and grey overhead. It was still too cold for insects. There were points of colour dotted around, the purples and yellows of weeds. A leveret was hiding in the ankle-length grass, being watched by the buzzard above.

Ursula sat and sketched. She was wearing an apricot wool hat.

The ground was cold but not wet. She had forgotten to bring a blanket and other practicalities, like a clip to hold the pages at the corners.

Ursula did not like landscapes. She didn't know or want to know the names of plants or birds or formations. It felt ostentatious to draw outdoors. Most of all she disliked the mental projection that landscapes involved. The fly tipping of the mind onto the landscape. The turning of the landscape into things. Into metaphors.

She sketched a few pictures to get her eye in and to find her rhythm and to warm up her fingers. As she finished each, she tore the pages off and lay them beside her with a rock weighing on top.

Ursula sat and looked at Ghost Mountain, while resting her hands in her lap. Ghost Mountain was unmoving and unconcealable and yet it was almost impossible to see clearly.

Ursula thought her sketches were juvenile. They looked like stupid sales graphs.

Rain started spotting her paper. The wind was so strong that it was shaking drops from the clouds. Ursula decided to take shelter in the abandoned Ghost Mountain house.

Ursula packed up her things as the rain intensified. She winced into the wind.

The back door to the house was unlocked and the lights still worked. There were odours in pungent competition with each other and the dirt was coated with dust. Ursula squeezed past junk-filled boxes, stacked above her own height. The house had been unoccupied ever since Christopher and his mother had left, years before, though it could never be truly empty of them in Ursula's eyes. She sought traces of them everywhere.

Looking out at Ghost Mountain through the kitchen window, she tried to sketch it from that viewpoint but she lacked the technical skill to depict glass. To depict something that was both there and not there.

Ursula lifted some musty blankets and sat in the old kitchen chair.

It was intense to feel Christopher brimming inside her and to feel Ghost Mountain outside, though the line between inside and outside was hardly real. Whether she herself was inside or outside or whether she was merely the boundary between the two, she could not say.

Ursula fell still and serious.

She would not be able to draw Ghost Mountain today.

Later that evening, back at her own house, she could not convey any of this to her housemates and their various boyfriends, who were all giddy with drinking. To them, it would sound like a boring drug dream. They were listening to music and the boyfriends were trying to better each other's jokes.

So Ursula texted her own boyfriend and took the crosstown train to stay at his house. She did girlfriend things to him, after which he slept well, while she lay awake and thought about how to draw glass.

How to deal with invisible boundaries.

Christopher

It was true that Christopher's business was a success and that he had some money, though he also had debts to match the money he made. He had learned that credit disguised failure as success. That a person who owned and owed a lot was viewed as rich whereas a person who owned and owed a little was considered poor. That a rich person was someone who had access to credit and that a poor person was someone who had no access to credit.

After they had left the Ghost Mountain house, Martha had rented an apartment and Christopher had rented a different, smaller, apartment. Though they could not afford separate accommodation, the rumours about their shared bed gave them no choice.

Martha's place was above the heel bar. When she asked about the rent, the kind owner of the heel bar asked her what she could afford, and so the rent was set. He offered her a job too. The heel bar owner explained that because people no longer bought shoes that could be repaired, they also cut keys and took in dry cleaning to keep the place going. Christopher did not know how dry cleaning worked or if it was truly dry. Martha took the job and the apartment. She had fully expected that the heel bar owner would attempt to take advantage of her and she had already decided that she would not resist him if he turned out to be what she expected. But he did not try that. One of the other employees did try that with her and lost his job. The heel bar owner fired the employee but paid him his next month's wages in advance so that the employee could start again. He did not want the employee acting out his disgruntlement on someone else. The heel bar owner knew that one thing led to another and that sometimes one thing prevented another.

Christopher lived in a small apartment. His bed was in the same room as his kitchen. There was a desk against the wall where he would sit and watch wrestling on his computer. He would watch fight highlights and in-character interviews. He did not care for documentaries about why wrestling was fake, or in which retired wrestlers talked about how they all took drugs.

Christopher knew his mother very well. He knew that when he started making money and then continued making money that it would make no difference to her. She would be happy that he had money if that's what he wanted, but that it was not what she was interested in. She thought money and worrying about money took up too much of people's lives and she did not see the sense of letting that problem intrude more than necessary. Her main concerns were her job at the heel bar and her apartment, into which she introduced small comforts. She was happy to work for the heel bar owner, who shared her priorities. He had enough money to open a second or third heel bar but instead was content with the single shop he owned. He often said to her that a person should not take up too much space in the world, which was how she felt too. A person could not be more honest than their boss and so Martha was glad to have an honest boss. She had once entertained warm thoughts about him but corrected herself. The heel bar owner was unattractive and while she was not above enjoying the mild perversion of desiring an ugly man, it was easier to think of him as one thing and one thing only. For his part, he too seemed to have arrived at the same conclusion, though presumably he was not above enjoying the perversion of desiring an attractive employee, which Martha most certainly was. He was above acting on it, however.

Christopher could have used the money from his business to introduce some luxury into his life. But, perhaps influenced by his mother's example, he did not want a bigger apartment. He had enough room to eat and sleep and watch wrestling comfortably. He did not want to bring anybody back to his apartment. He did not need to project to the world that he had money or that he had credit. Instead, he continued to spend the same amount of money he had always spent, perhaps even a little less, as he revelled in discovering new minor household economies. He did not revel in the parsimony but in the simplification. That he had identified something unnecessary and eliminated it. This, to him, seemed what nature itself would do in his situation.

His only luxury was that he would watch wrestling videos late into the night even when he had an early start the next morning. It was not the violence or the adrenalin that he enjoyed, but the stories.

After he had watched wrestling, he would lie in his bed and observe that by living simply, there was less space for absences. Less space for the absence of Ursula.

Trampolines

Christopher had been a tall child but was a not-very-tall young man. He had stopped growing around the time his father abandoned him on the couch with his father's girlfriend's children. As far as Christopher knew, his father was no longer with that woman or her children.

But Christopher appreciated that feelings about fathers were not something a person could pick or choose. They were not a matter of policy.

He asked his mother about it one evening over dinner at a steakhouse.

Martha stabbed her fork into her steak and said it was ironic that his father loved maps so much but nobody ever knew where he was. She said that summed him up beautifully.

Christopher understood his mother's hard feelings, though it surprised him to see how provoked she was. A lot of time had passed and, as a beautiful woman, she had not been short of male attention. She continued to say how she didn't want to talk about it but, as she chewed her steak with tenacity, Christopher could tell she was really chewing her thoughts about his father.

The time Christopher had called to see his father, he had been wearing the uniform of the crosstown train company. In the complex way of things, this got to Christopher. The driver of the crosstown train was the kind of job any boy would want for his father. It was a romantic job. It had paternal connotations.

Ever since the steakhouse conversation with his mother, the crosstown train had been on Christopher's mind. When he arrived at the station, he didn't know how the ticketing system worked and he didn't understand which platform took passengers across the city and which ones took them back. And of course, he had no idea which was his father's train, assuming he still drove one or ever had. Christopher guessed that there were multiple trains in circulation at any given time and that with rostering and so on, he could travel on the crosstown system many times without ever encountering his father.

He boarded at the last carriage, farthest from the driver. His gaze followed a fly that had flown onto the train and which was now bumping against the window. It would probably stay aboard the train for the rest of its life, not understanding why it could never leave.

The view from his seat gave him a different perspective on the town. Travelling by crosstown train took you on a tour of people's back gardens, whereas the roads showed frontage only. Christopher was surprised to learn that so many people had trampolines. They must have to clean bird dirt from them and sweep them every now and then. After a rain shower, the children would not be able to bounce around until the surface was dry again.

The train stalled on a bridge that crossed a busy road and was stationary for several minutes. After some time, a four-note scale was played over the speaker, catching the passengers' attention, including Christopher's. The driver blew on the microphone. In a nasal voice he explained the cause of the delay.

But the cause and extent of the delay did not interest Christopher. At the sound of the voice of some other man who was not his father, the crosstown train and the journey and the back gardens and the trampolines all became one blurred nothing.

Preferences

Ursula and her boyfriend had a pendular bed life that alternated between her preferences and his preferences.

Her preferences were tactile and intimate.

His were verbal and energetic.

He ran hot last thing at night. She ran hot in the mornings. He liked it when he had been drinking a little. She liked to feel rested and fresh.

She didn't mind his preferences, though afterwards she sometimes felt shy at the things she had said. She didn't know what he thought of her preferences. That everything moved too slowly, probably.

Ursula often felt detached during their lovemaking. It always felt like there was something else in the room with them. Afterwards she would wonder whether there was something wrong with her.

Late one night, she began to cry quietly beside him, thinking he was asleep. She rested her forearm across her eyebrows. Tears leaked under her closed eyelids and ran down her unhappy laughter lines.

He cleared back her fringe and kissed her forehead. He wiped her nose and waited for her to speak first.

But Ursula had no explanation to give him.

She had not cried in a long time.

And now she wasn't sure if she was crying for herself or for Christopher, whom she had shockingly seen on the train on the way to her boyfriend's place. She saw him and almost faked that she hadn't. She had frozen in his calm, sad gaze. He simply looked at her, unembarrassed to be seen crying quietly to himself.

And thinking about it all now in bed, reminded her of how much she had missed him those past few years, and how seeing him reopened the gap inside her that she had tried so hard to grow around.

Foot Splinter

The following weekend, Ursula sat outside on a foldable stool and again tried to sketch Ghost Mountain. After many attempts at drawing it in the centre of the page, she tried instead placing it in the bottom right-hand corner. It seemed happier there. In the expanse of white paper that this liberated, she drew the swifts that were flying fast and low around her, picking-off cow pat insects. She used as few strokes of the pencil as were barely necessary, though each stroke seemed like one too many.

The swifts looked like shurikens in her picture. Ursula rubbed them with the flat of her thumb to make them blurry. To give them movement. It dirtied the page and ruined the sketch.

A veil of rain hung between Ghost Mountain and the horizon. It was travelling towards her. She packed up and sought shelter again in the Ghost Mountain house.

From inside, Ursula watched the wind as it bent the rain. She could see that she had left her apricot hat behind in the grass. The wool would be ruined.

Ursula had been so close to capturing her picture but then she had lost it. Lost it in the details. It was not her technical proficiency that was wanting. Not her eyes and not her fingers. She could draw something that looked like Ghost Mountain but she could not draw something that felt like Ghost Mountain.

The rain that had seemed to be visiting was now clearly staying.

As she looked out at her apricot hat, she imagined Christopher walking there with a dog of his own. Christopher's corkscrew hair dark and flattened with wetness. The dog with a tennis ball in its jaws.

More than anything, she wanted to believe in the possibility of Christopher's contentedness.

She could have drawn it in a matter of moments. Her pencil would hardly have needed to lift from the page.

Perhaps she went to Ghost Mountain so she could affect surprise if he appeared. He would discover her at her best. He would discover her with her sketchbook, immersed in something that wasn't him. And this would make Christopher think that it was his thrill to discover her, and not hers to be discovered by him.

They would shelter together in the Ghost Mountain house, where they would remove their wet boots and heavy socks.

And if, walking barefoot around those rooms, she suffered a splinter in her foot, Christopher would prise it free gently, using his teeth if his fingers failed. And she would look down proudly upon his tenderness.

Potato

As Elaine got older her body had become less tolerant. Her body was tyrannical in its lack of tolerance.

If she stayed out in the sun for too long she would get dizzy and her temples would pound.

If she ate too much or too late, her insides would churn and cramp.

Her body would tire more easily but when she rested it, it punished her by stretching her nights into a long sleepless labyrinth of worries.

She was ever thirsty but whatever she drank, her body processed in multiples, only for her thirst to return, unslaked.

Elaine's afternoon nap became deeper and she would now have a morning nap too. She would cock her head back, relieving the weight from her spine, and breathe through her mouth. She often woke herself with her own snoring, though Dominic never complained about it. Her interlaced fingers would rest on the buckle of her belt and her thumbs would touch. The warmth of her hands on her abdomen would bring her comfort. She would wake to find that her hands were resting under her jumper. That the skin of her tummy needed to feel their tactile attention.

Elaine respected her body. It had cared for her. It was knowledgeable about itself. There was so much she did not know about it. On the most inactive of days, it would have done so much without her even realising. Elaine's body had a wordless way of communicating its troubles to her.

She would say to Dominic, "I think I'll have the rest of that curry tomorrow," about a curry that she used to be able to finish.

And she would say, "I'm cold. Are you cold?"

During the night she would visit and revisit the bathroom and lie awake in her room, longing for company. In her loneliness, she would stand on the landing outside his room, listening to him breathing, and whisper, "Are you awake, Dominic?"

But Dominic would still be sleeping on his stomach. And Elaine would once again remind herself to share with him her theory that the reason his eyebrow hairs curled so much was because he slept face down.

Elaine observed these changes in her body. She lay in her bed palpating her stomach to feel from the outside what felt like a hard potato just under her belly button.

"Oh," she thought.

That night, Elaine did not think about Life or Death. Instead, Elaine asked, "Where is my art?" She wondered, "What was all that painting for if not for this? If not for now?"

The thought made her feel abandoned. It frightened her.

At breakfast, Dominic was reading the news on his phone. He had made Elaine her coffee but she couldn't drink it. She told him she was considering switching to tea. Herbal tea, even.

She had drunk coffee all her life.

"I was thinking," she said. "Maybe you should get a dog."

Dominic stopped scrolling on his phone and looked at Elaine over his glasses.

"I should get a dog?" he repeated.

"Yes," she said.

"What for?" he asked.

"In case you get lonely."

"I thought you said you couldn't bear to lose another dog?" he said.

Elaine could feel everything swirling inside her gut. Swirling around the hard potato.

"I'm not well. I think it might be my time," she said sadly.

Dominic reached over and stroked her knuckles.

"I want you to know," she said, "That I could not have been more loved."

Portrait

When Elaine woke the next morning, Dominic was lying beside her. He would spend every night in her single bed from then on.

Dominic asked her to teach him how to paint. He said he only wanted to learn how to paint people, not landscapes.

Elaine told him, "It doesn't work like that."

Dominic said, "But lots of people start to paint at an older age."

"It's not age," said Elaine. "You have to learn how to see first. It's a way of looking, not just painting."

"Well then, you can be my eyes," said Dominic.

He took down her paintings from the attic. Elaine had asked him to destroy them long ago. She had said that they weren't good enough and they weren't going to get any better. But he had kept them.

Dominic held up the portrait she had made of him with his teeth missing. The one Ursula had ruined.

In the picture, his elbows were on the chair and his hand hung casually over the edge. He was wearing double denim and the button over his abdomen was undone. Though it wasn't a flattering portrait, or a good likeness, he said it looked poignant. He pronounced it "pwog-nant."

Elaine had no time for poignancy. She thought poignancy was manipulative.

The painting was better than Elaine had remembered, but smaller too. It was a matter of regret for her that she had painted her pictures so small. It was because she had worried about money and felt guilty about buying paint when Ursula needed clothes for school and Dominic still hadn't had his teeth fixed. Her pictures were smaller and used fewer colours because of this. Perhaps that was why the creative rain had abandoned her. Either that or the fact that she had kissed Ocho in his sleep before he died on Ghost Mountain. She often thought about that.

Elaine did not want to teach Dominic how to paint because that meant that she too would have to paint. She could not lift a brush unless it was to give form to creative rain. She respected herself too much and respected creative rain too much to paint any other way.

All those years when she had been barren artistically, she had assumed for no reason that if she waited loyally, creative rain would return. And so, she tried not to begrudge its departure, nor blame it for its absence. Now, with the hard potato in her gut, she had expected that the creative rain would play some part in an artistic denouement. But the creative rain was as mysterious as always. It was not hers or anybody's and did not behave as it might be wished to behave.

Creative rain did not believe in poignancy.

Bus Change

Elaine said she was worried that Ursula would undergo a crisis because of the hard potato in Elaine's gut.

Ursula said, "I know everyone dies. I really do. I know that I will die and that Dominic will die and that you will die."

Ursula didn't say that she had learned this from being the last person to look directly at Ocho before he died. The day she had learned what death looked like.

Dominic stroked Ursula's cheek with the back of his fingers.

Elaine kissed Ursula's hair and said, "I know, I know."

When Ursula returned to her house and lay on her bed, her housemate slipped a note under her bedroom door asking if Ursula had been the one who touched the coins that were left on the kitchen table, and that if she was, could she return them and no more would be said about it.

Ursula wanted to cry and cry and cry but there was a knot in her throat. She pictured it like a goitre. It was as if she had not chewed her sadness sufficiently and now it was stuck.

She rang her boyfriend and told him about Elaine's hard potato and the goitre. Ursula's boyfriend said he knew how she felt. His grandmother had died from something similar. He didn't say which grandmother. He was young at the time. His grandmother had a large lump on her neck. Her death caused great confusion for him.

Ursula clarified that she was the one with the goitre feeling. Elaine had a hard potato in her gut. She said she wasn't confused. Everyone would die. She would die and so would her boyfriend. Ursula said she was absolutely certain about that.

Her boyfriend invited her over.

Ursula took the bus to avoid using the crosstown train. To avoid seeing Christopher again. She paid using the coins she had taken from the kitchen table earlier. She sat at the front of the bus on the upper level. The trees had been growing and scratched against the bus windows. The bus vibrated and swayed. Inside, her body also vibrated and swayed.

Ursula lay on her boyfriend's single bed and talked uninter-rupted for a long time, though not really about Elaine. She noticed herself doing this and wondered whether it was a response to shocking news. To avoid a crisis, she was shoring-up a newly-rent hole in the side of her life with any alternative information she could find. Trying to make her life about something else, anything else.

Ursula's boyfriend ran his fingers through her hair like a rake. It calmed her scalp. She hadn't realised that her scalp needed such comfort. Then she noticed other parts of her body that were sad. Her jaw was sad and so too was the tongue in her mouth. When a person was in crisis, she thought that perhaps the distinction between their body and mind collapsed and they finally inhabited their body. Usually, it felt like her mind was something that lived in her body but in a separated way. Like her body was an apartment block and her mind was her apartment.

Ursula had momentarily forgotten where she was. Having her scalp raked had made her daydreamy.

Her boyfriend said he had heard about a place called Weeping Mountain and that they could visit sometime and stay overnight there. That people found it a healing place. That it had healing energy. That even if she didn't believe in that sort of thing, it worked anyway.

Ursula had heard of Weeping Mountain before. Old people went there to pray and desperate people brought their sick family members there. It was a hokey tourist place. The water that wept from the mountain was from a seasonal underground source. The people who bottled and sold it were charlatans.

Ursula's boyfriend had grown up in a camping family. They had money alright but they enjoyed camping because it was outdoors and authentic and because of nature. They saw nature as something separate from themselves and better too. Ursula had never met his parents but she could imagine them easily. His father would be tall and professorial. His mother would be the one who held everything together. He was probably friends with his parents, but not to the extent that he would tell them his boyfriend preferences.

As she lay in her boyfriend's arms, she could tell that he was getting aroused from being squashed in the single bed. It didn't bother her. Ursula knew that people could be sincere and still have an oblivious body, so she stroked his stomach and kissed him. Then she girlfriended him. She felt better afterwards. The intimacy was worth it. It unlocked her body. She had been curious whether her crying would be unlocked when the rest of her body was unlocked, but that was not what happened. The goitre feeling remained.

Weeping Mountain

That weekend Ursula's boyfriend took her camping at Weeping Mountain. She met him outside his building after work on the Friday. He had gone to the office wearing hiking boots and a warm fleece and carrying a backpack. Lots of people leaving his office wore those sorts of clothes even though they worked at computers and weren't going camping.

His enthusiasm at showing her the boot of the car and everything he had thought to bring reminded her that she hated camping enthusiasm. That this healing weekend was no longer about her crisis and had become about his love of camping. Or his remembered love of camping. He had not done it since he was a child. He had never even been to a music festival.

He set up the tent quickly even though it was windy and even though it looked to Ursula like a two-person job. She stood there and watched, holding the tent pegs he had given her to mind. There were a couple of other tents, all respectfully distanced from each other. The people were not neighbourly but they weren't rude either. They were most likely getting away from things and didn't want it spoiled by camping small talk. Her boyfriend said that this was the place where real campers went. The tourist types camped on the leeward side where the toilets were.

Ursula climbed into the tent after him.

"It's bigger than you think, isn't it?" he said, hunching over as he walked in a small circle.

Ursula lay back on her sleeping bag. The ground beneath her was lumpy. Small rocks protruded and Ursula could feel them against her tailbone.

"If there's one thing camping teaches you it's that there is no such thing as flat ground," he said. The observation clearly pleased him. He said it in a way that implied there was a lot more where that came from.

He offered to make her beans on toast using the gas stove, but Ursula had brought a sandwich from the deli with her, so he made it for himself only. This satisfied him as though he had hunted and killed the beans himself.

The tent was stuffy so Ursula slept near the zip end.

Her boyfriend slept deeply behind her. He had said that if there's one thing camping teaches you it's that fresh air helps you sleep better. So far that was two things that camping taught you.

Ursula stared out into the dark that was truly dark. Her hood was up and her sleeping bag was zipped as far as it would go. She spat when an insect landed in her mouth.

Ursula got a fright when a man tripped over their guy ropes. He wasn't aware of her presence and whisper-cursed to himself. She withdrew her head into the tent and zipped it closed.

The man was feeling his way past the tent with difficulty. He was whisper-shouting someone's name. He must have lost his bearings when he went to pee in the bushes and now he couldn't find his way back to his tent. Again, he whisper-shouted his friend's name. He wanted them to whisper shout back so he could figure out which direction to head in, like campsite sonar.

Ursula turned on her torch so that the dim glow would help him navigate the tent. She wondered whether she should have kept one of the tent pegs in her sleeping bag in case she got attacked.

After he had gone, she took out her book and read by torchlight. In the stillness she could hear the dull friction of insects against the outside of the tent, drawn to the light source. She had been reading the same book for weeks. It was not making any impression on her and whenever it was not in her hand she forgot it even existed. An old woman was dying in the book and even though Elaine was dying too, the book still bored her.

She woke early as the sun baked her through the polyester.

Her boyfriend was already awake and making coffee on his little gas stove. He had brought some seed bread and bananas for breakfast. He broke off some seed bread and handed it to her. Ursula wondered if and where he had washed his hands.

He was cheerful and pointed out what he said was a nuthatch flying in and out of a hole in what he said was a larch tree.

It sounded like a line from a poem he had learned and which he was dying to recite.

His legs were crossed and he wore shorts.

Ursula wore the skinny jeans she had slept in and white running shoes that used to be white. She alternated between a bite of banana and a bite of seed bread, one in each hand. As she swallowed, she again noticed the goitre feeling. This reminded her of her crisis and of Elaine.

They walked around to the leeward side. There was a track at the foot of Weeping Mountain where there were kiosks selling coffee and pastries and bottles of Weeping Mountain water. Ursula didn't know whether you were meant to drink the water or wash in it or spray it on whatever or whomever you wanted to protect.

There was a campsite with about fifty tents and a gentle buzz of activity around the place. Ursula and her boyfriend had risen early to get ahead of the busyness, but camping people were all like-minded that way so everyone else had got up early too.

The track to the summit was wide and gentle to begin with but soon turned into a narrow stony zig-zag. Some couples had brought fibreglass sticks but there were also parents in shorts carrying children on their shoulders. Ursula's boyfriend held her hand initially but released it once the gradient got steeper and his footing required some thought.

The day was bright but it was still too early for the heat to have cooked the air. There was something chirping in the gorse. It was somewhere between an insect and a bird noise. It was a single voice but Ursula could not tell which direction it was coming from. She could not see how the noise could be described as a song. It had the personality of an electronic noise. Like an alarm clock or a microwave.

Her boyfriend stopped halfway to look at the view.

A single shadow moved across the fields, cast by a cloud above. Ursula watched it until it was absorbed by a larger shade.

"Some day you'll have to come up here and paint that," said her boyfriend.

Ursula wasn't sure what he thought painting was.

At the summit, they sat on a flat, bald patch of ground and let the wind make sea sounds in their earholes. It was a calm day but at the summit there was still some violence in the way the air moved. It was not hard to imagine a child being blown over the edge.

People were taking photos on their phones. A group of men was kneeling and saying prayers. A young couple were kissing – the girl was on her tiptoes and had her hands in the boy's jean pockets. An unaccompanied dog was digging his nose beneath a flat stone.

People were waiting for the weeping.

"Do they know when the weeping starts? Is it like a geyser or something?" asked Ursula.

"No. At this time of year it all depends on whether it has been raining lately. It's a flooding thing."

"What if the rain washes away the tents?"

"That won't happen," he said, though he didn't explain why.

A gathering formed on the far side of the summit so Ursula and her boyfriend joined it. A woman with a fibreglass stick pointed out a dark stain on the rocks and gorse below them.

"There is water coming from that swallow hole, see?" she said.

Ursula couldn't see anything.

"Does it not come out stronger than that?" asked Ursula.

"It's not here to entertain us – it's not Seaworld!" said her boyfriend, like a performing seal himself, for the woman's benefit, betraying Ursula.

They could see that the mountain was leaking, alright.

Some parents were trying to generate excitement for the kids by saying, "Look! Look! The mountain is crying," but there was anti-climax in their voices.

On the journey down, Ursula's boyfriend told her to walk sideways down the uneven bits, so she would be more secure if she slipped. An older man had walked ahead of her and skinned his shin when he skidded on a loose rock. She lifted his hat from where it fell and returned it to him.

At the bottom of the mountain, they left the leeward side behind and took the muddy track back through the trees to where their tent was. Her boyfriend was quiet and did not point out any nuthatches or larches.

When they arrived back to their base, all the other tents had gone. There was a young boy standing outside their tent on his phone. His dog was on a leash looking inside the tent. The boy was about fourteen years old but the size of a man. He had a moustache that was like an eyebrow on his lip.

Ursula's boyfriend dropped his bag and walked at pace to the boy.

"What's the big idea?" said her boyfriend aggressively. He cursed the dog and he cursed the boy. He asked where the boy's parents were.

The boy was looking at him calmly. They were about the same height, though the boy was bulkier.

Ursula's boyfriend yanked the leash from the boy's hand and pulled the dog out roughly. The dog made a strained coughing sound.

The boy put Ursula's boyfriend in a headlock and they struggled wordlessly for a few moments. Then the dog started barking and Ursula's boyfriend kicked out at it with a wild leg, missing it by so much that the dog didn't even flinch. The boy was walking in circles with Ursula's boyfriend in the headlock. Ursula didn't know what would happen next. She didn't think the boy did either. He was in control and it was up to him what would happen to her boyfriend.

Eventually the boy released him and Ursula's boyfriend staggered backwards a little. The boy walked calmly towards him and headbutted Ursula's boyfriend before turning and walking off with his dog.

Ursula crouched down beside her boyfriend whose mouth was gushing. He was looking in amazement at his two front teeth in the palm of his bloody hand.

Childhood

Christopher was making a lot of money. He had discovered that when you weren't important you were paid for your work and that when you were important you were paid for your decisions. He was paid for his decisions. Because he didn't care so much about money, he didn't care about the decisions and so they were easy to make. When people saw him make important decisions lightly they thought it was because he knew what he was doing.

People said about Christopher that he had a brilliant business brain.

It was because he made so much money while still being so young.

But in his heart, Christopher had contempt for business. He thought it was stupid that a person could ask for other people's money. He thought it stupid that the people who lent him the money respected him more than he respected them or their money.

Christopher was still living in his small apartment and watching wrestling. Because he had nothing to spend his money on, he used it to borrow more money.

This meant that the more money he made the poorer and poorer he got.

He called to the heel bar, where his mother worked. He wanted her to restore his equilibrium. He had been out of equilibrium since failing to hear his father's voice on the train and instead, seeing Ursula.

Christopher sat on a high stool. A man sat in the stool next to him, waiting for Martha to cut him a new set of keys. The man on the stool looked at Martha with eyes of love. Martha was beautiful and was used to this. Christopher had never got used to this.

The man asked Martha if she would like to have a drink with him sometime. Martha said "No, thanks," and handed the man his keys.

The man asked if he could have some coloured rubber covers for his keys so he would be able to tell which was which. Martha said, "On the house," as she handed them to him.

After he had left, Christopher told his mother what had happened on the train, all about his father and Ursula, and about what he had been doing with his money. He always told Martha everything. There were no secrets between them.

"You need to stop boiling your childhood," she said to him.

Christopher denied that was what he was doing, though he liked the phrase.

The phrase was so descriptive it made him wonder, "Have I been boiling my childhood?"

He asked his mother. He said: "Do you boil your parenthood?"

And she said, "No. I did a great job."

She was wearing her safety glasses and was working on some keys. She didn't flinch at all when they sparked. Martha had highly-trained powers of concentration. She said that was where she got her equilibrium from. That a person needed to be able to concentrate to be happy.

That night, Christopher made some macaroni and cheese and watched wrestling. As the pasta boiled Christopher was once again reminded of his mother's phrase. He continued to think about it as he chewed his pasta and watched the wrestler apply a move called the Camel Clutch. There was no getting out of the Camel Clutch.

Again, he thought, "Have I been boiling my childhood?"

He noticed that the lemon in his fruit bowl had become mouldy in its southern hemisphere. The top half was fine. He cut it in two and sucked the good half to see if it was OK.

Christopher did not have his mother's concentration. His mind would transition from his childhood to a Camel Clutch to a lemon hemisphere. His mind was a boiling mind.

That night, after dinner, he rode the train across town and back for no reason. It had become a new habit of his. As he rode the train for no reason, his mind boiled for his father's voice, and it boiled for a glimpse of Ursula.

Equilibrium

Christopher had been thinking about his equilibrium.

He thought about what was present in his life when he was in equilibrium that was missing when his life was not in equilibrium. There were two things missing: Ursula and Ghost Mountain.

Christopher called to the solicitor's office and asked them what they knew about Ghost Mountain. He wanted to know who owned it and whether they would sell it to him. He said he wanted to buy it, without first asking how much it would cost. That's how little he was interested in money.

The solicitor explained that the land was owned by the estate of the former owner, may he rest in peace. The solicitor was acting as executrix.

Christopher asked what that meant? Who owned the estate?

The solicitor explained that, as she was the executrix, she had a fiduciary duty to preserve the estate's best interests but that, in the ordinary sense of the word, ownership did not vest in any known physical person but in a legal entity, that being the estate of the former owner, may he rest in peace.

It was explained to Christopher that land – specifically, a mountain – could be owned not only by a person but by a legal construct. That most tangible expression of physicality could itself be subject to something that had no physical manifestation. A piece of paper could hold unassailable rights over a mountain.

In order to acquire the land and the mountain, Christopher would need to make that piece of paper happy. To do right by it. The executrix was duty bound to see to no other outcome.

Christopher asked how much money the piece of paper would want for the mountain.

The solicitor, acting as executrix, said that a valuation would be required.

Christopher asked how they would value a mountain. What were its alternative uses?

The solicitor explained that it had existence value and vicarious value, as well as agricultural value and recreational value. There was also a small house attached. A second house had been rented out when the landlord was alive, but it had been sold after the landlord's death, when the tenant had absconded.

Christopher said he knew the small house. He had lived there. He realised now that the piece of paper had been his landlord.

The executrix had a valuation done, which was for more than Christopher could afford, but not more than he could borrow. He would make the piece of paper very rich.

It took a few weeks for the formalities to be finalised. The piece of paper was fastidious in its dealings. While everything was being organised, Christopher would drive out to the land and sit on the wall he knew so well and look out on Ghost Mountain, which nobody could claim to know fully, never mind understand.

The transaction had distracted him from his business and he made decisions even more carelessly than usual. The business had bought him what he really wanted and it was of no further interest to him now. The questions that came to him did not require much thought. They were questions of approval. People who worked for him would seek his approval for a particular course of action and he would agree without probing into the details.

Christopher walked to the top of Ghost Mountain and surveyed the surrounding landscape, just as he had done as a boy. Just as he had done when he would keep watch for the return of his father. His habit had been to pick a point on the horizon and select it as his father's place of work. From there he would track the movement of any distant human form he could make out, and imagine they were walking home to Ghost Mountain.

As he looked down at the house from the summit, he understood that his ambition had not been to own Ghost Mountain and its house, but to walk up to his father and his mother and Ursula and declare that he had bought it for them all.

Christopher spent the night at the Ghost Mountain house, his new house.

As his mind wandered into realms, he thought he could feel the presence of Ghost Mountain, or maybe it was just his own equilibrium.

Wrestling

When Christopher looked through the greasy window of the house the next morning, he saw Ursula painting at the foot of Ghost Mountain. Her picture was clipped to a wooden board. She dabbed her brush on her tongue from time to time. He could not see what she was painting. Without inhibition, he approached her and watched from behind, a dozen footsteps or so away. He had been standing there for more than a quarter of an hour before she addressed him, without turning around.

"Would you mind moving that litter please – it's in the scene."

There was a clump of congealed matter about twenty feet in the distance.

Christopher passed her and approached it.

"It's a dead leveret," he called.

"Leave it, so," she said.

He walked back towards her.

"Even if it's dead, if it's from here, it belongs in the picture," she explained.

"I didn't look at your painting, by the way" he said and returned to the house.

From inside, he continued to watch her painting. On his phone he had many missed calls and texts. Each one was a decision yearning to be made. They would become more difficult the longer they went unmade.

At lunchtime he brought her out some food on a plate – brioche and a banana, some cashew nuts and an apple that rolled around – then returned to his chair in the kitchen.

He came back an hour later and brought the plate away. Without interrupting her brushwork, she said, "Thank you, Christopher."

At dinner time, he made her beans and boiled an egg. He left her the rest of the brioche and said he would go to the shop if necessary. Again, absorbed in her painting, she thanked him but continued working.

Christopher ate alone in the kitchen. He ate beans from the pot and boiled two eggs. Afterwards he had the rest of the apples. They had been grown too quickly and were watery with no flavour.

As the sun dimmed, he saw Ursula sitting still for a long time. He wasn't sure whether she was looking at her painting or Ghost Mountain or both. She stood up and kicked over the easel she had been working from and crumpled up the picture she had just finished. She also collected the completed pictures she had been working on all day and mashed them together as if to make a snowball. In her anger she was making body noises. Not words as such, but guttural exorcistic sounds.

Christopher watched as she tramped back towards the house. He held the door open for her and relieved her of her easel, which he leaned against the kitchen chair. Ursula ran the kitchen tap for a long time before testing the water's temperature with her dirty fingers, and then gulping back a pint glass of it.

"You can stay here tonight," said Christopher.

"I know," said Ursula, and went into the bedroom and started taking off her boots and her jeans.

"You can stay too," she called from the bedroom. "But I'll only be sleeping, just so you know."

Christopher joined her in the bedroom tentatively. She was under the covers and was wearing a t-shirt that was old and stretched at the neck. Her eyes were closed. Christopher didn't usually sleep until two or three. It took him that long to unwind, especially if he had been watching wrestling.

He lay on his stomach above the sheets. He had taken off his boots and his socks but not his jeans. His shirt was draped over the back of a chair.

Ursula lay still and it was hard to tell whether she was asleep or pretending. Christopher was a restless sleeper. Eventually his breathing slowed and his mind began to shift from thinking to wandering into realms.

His dreams that night were coherent and plausible but not relevant.

When he woke the next morning he was lying across the bed, alone. He heard breakfast noises. Wind was leaking through the window frame and his forearms were chilly.

He stood in the doorway and scratched his pigeon chest. Ursula had already been working on a new painting. He admired the picture. It spoke to him.

Ursula said, "It's called 'Wrestling.'"

Christopher could see that there were two young men. One had the other in a headlock. Even though their faces were not filled in, and in fact were smeared, he could tell that the dominant one was younger than the other. Ursula had painted their positions with attentiveness. Any wrestling fan could see that. The turn of the hips and the shoulders were just right. Though the painting was static it was full of movement. It was not hard to imagine what had come before the action and what might come next. Christopher was very moved.

"I thought you were painting Ghost Mountain?" he said.

"I thought that too, but I couldn't do it. It's beyond me. I'm not ready for it."

Christopher poured himself some of the coffee Ursula had made. He went to top up her coffee mug but it had brushes in it.

"I didn't even know you liked wrestling," he said.

"Elaine says that painting is seeing," said Ursula. "The guy in the headlock is my boyfriend. This really happened."

"It looks like it really happened," said Christopher.

Ursula moved the picture against the wall.

"I can't go anywhere until that's dry," she said.

"You can stay here," said Christopher.

"That's what I was planning to do. I'm almost out of money," said Ursula. "But we can't both stay here."

"You can stay here," said Christopher, again.

So Ursula decided to leave the house she had been sharing to move into the Ghost Mountain house. She returned her housemate's bus change, which she had taken from the kitchen table. One of the students she had been sharing with took Ursula's old room because it was larger. The student moved in with her boyfriend, who had skinny bald calves.

Elaine is not cold

Elaine was thinking about being sick and about dying.

Earlier that morning, Dominic had said that he was scared for them both. She said back to him that after it was all over, she would no longer be experiencing experiences, so he should only be sad for himself. She would not even be experiencing the missing of experiences. There was no need to ever say, "Elaine would have loved this" or "It's a shame Elaine is missing this."

As she was explaining everything she thought, "Am I cold? Is this a cold thing to think?"

But it was not a cold thing to think.

Elaine asked him what he would do afterwards.

Dominic said he would join a monastery. Or he would go back to being the town drunk.

Elaine replied, "You're only saying that in the hope that I will stop you, or that it will make me change my mind about dying."

Elaine knew that Dominic would struggle and that he did not have coping skills. But she also knew that he was at his worst when he was being indulged.

After their conversation, Dominic left to help Ursula move her things into the Ghost Mountain house. Elaine could hardly believe that Ursula was moving back there, of all places. "Surely there are other houses in the world?" Elaine had said.

But Elaine understood.

Ursula had offered to move in to their house to help care for Elaine. She said that even though she didn't know how to care for her, she would learn. That she would help Dominic.

It had hurt Ursula when Elaine said no.

Elaine did not explain to Ursula that her dying instinct had become strong and that the process of retreating was already underway. It was a mistake to work against the flow of things. It was better to see where things were going and to get there first.

She knew that her death was complicated for Ursula. She asked Ursula if she wanted to talk about it, but Ursula said, "I completely understand that you will die and Dominic will die and I will die."

And Elaine believed her even though Ursula was still so young and did not yet know that understanding something was only the start of it and not the end.

Elaine was surprised at how strong her dying instinct was. It was as though she had died before. As an artist, she had thought about death a lot. Elaine did not know why artists thought about death so much. Perhaps it was because of creative rain. But if making art was so much like dying, why had creative rain abandoned her?

This was the loneliest question of all.

Boyfriend

Dominic helped Ursula to load the car. There were black sacks of clothes, a few boxes of books, a wok, her painting of Spain, the food she hadn't yet eaten – including her spices – a desk chair and two lamps that weren't hers, but which she always liked. She explained to Dominic that the Ghost Mountain house was bare but it had furniture and other essentials. She didn't need much.

"I'll wait here if you want to say your goodbyes," said Dominic from behind the wheel.

"It's fine. Let's just go," said Ursula.

When they arrived at the Ghost Mountain house, the front door was locked so Dominic asked Ursula for the keys. She said she didn't have keys. The house was abandoned, so she was claiming it. If anyone asked she would say she was an artist on retreat there. The question of who was paying for the electricity that still worked went unexplored and unanswered.

Dominic sat in the old kitchen chair and looked out upon Ghost Mountain through the greasy glass.

"Is this one of yours?" he asked when he noticed the painting of the two young men wrestling.

"I feel like that's the first real painting I've ever done," said Ursula.

"Are you going to paint Ghost Mountain while you're here?"

"No. I've tried that. It can't be done. At least, not by me."

Ursula unwrapped the food they had brought and they ate an improvised lunch of bread rolls, apples and nuts. She made coffee for herself, but Dominic had switched to herbal tea in solidarity with Elaine, who could no longer drink coffee because of the hard potato in her gut.

They changed the sheets on the bed and Dominic asked Ursula about Elaine. About what Ursula thought would happen next and what she thought would happen afterwards. Dominic told her about his plans to either join a monastery or resume his role as the town drunk.

"You can't go back to being the town drunk," she said. "It's just some fantasy you have about when your life was simpler. It was also before I was born, so if you do that it would be like you were trying to erase me, too."

Dominic agreed not to revert to being the town drunk.

"And no monastery would let you in," continued Ursula. "They have rules about not admitting people who have been recently bereaved. Too many grieving people have gone into monasteries and had nervous breakdowns. They don't want that hassle. They don't want people ruining their buzz."

This made sense to Dominic. He would be the same. If he lived in a monastery he wouldn't want people ruining his buzz either.

He realised they were talking about him rather than Elaine. He understood that Elaine and Ursula had probably discussed him. Elaine would have asked her to watch out for him. If it were up to him alone, he would have liked to have shared the Ghost Mountain house with Ursula and leave their family home to their memories of Elaine. But Dominic did not want to become a burden to Ursula. She was young and he could see that even a loving daughter like Ursula would eventually find his company a chore. And anyway, after the scandal of Christopher and his mother sharing a bed in the house, it would be impossible for a parent and child to ever stay there together without invoking similar controversy.

"My boyfriend is en route," said Ursula, answering a text. "He's cycling here."

Dominic suddenly felt in the way. He guessed he would feel in the way a lot in the years to come.

The prospect of the boyfriend's imminent arrival had shifted the room chemistry and their conversation went quiet.

They stood and looked through the greasy window, anticipating the boyfriend's arrival.

When he came, they watched him struggle to lock his bike to the front gate, which then meant that he couldn't get through the gate easily. It made him seem uncoordinated.

Dominic was assessing the boyfriend. He had the height of a man but the body of a boy. His front was flat and his arms were thin. He hunched a little as though he was not yet ready to claim his full height.

Ursula let her boyfriend in and introduced him to her father.

As Dominic went to shake his hand they both smiled and saw that each was missing front teeth. It salved Dominic's new loneliness that Ursula had chosen a boyfriend who was like him in some way. He wondered if Ursula still had the front teeth he had given her all those years ago.

They made conversation and the boyfriend talked too much. He said he had got lost and that the mountain had not turned out to be a good landmark as it had different sides and the house had turned out to be on the last of them. He laughed as he told his story, though when he saw Dominic laughing, he instinctively lowered his top lip to cover his missing teeth.

He had been mid-laugh when he saw, leaning against the wall, the wrestling painting. He froze and said, "Is that ... Is that me?"

The boyfriend waited until Dominic had left before he broke up with Ursula.

Accident

Christopher had been neglectful of his business. They had missed the deadline for important Government tenders because he had not cleared the documentation and they were in trouble with the regulator for not responding to information requests.

In the previous weeks, one of his managers had been poached by another company. The manager had been responsible for a new quarry they had acquired. They had planned to blast and mine it before turning it into an overflow for the town dump, which was at capacity. It would be a lucrative project that would make money at every stage.

The manager had run a team of people, each of whom was expert in their own part of the job, but none of whom had enough management experience to run the project in its entirety. There was a terrible accident and a man was badly injured when the quarry was being blasted. He had lost his arms and his face was now unrecognisable. Would never again be recognisable. He was certainly blind and they would not know how much intellectual functioning he would retain until after he emerged from the induced coma they had put him in.

The police had not yet become involved and Christopher's team pleaded with him to speak to the man's wife to see if it could be handled quietly.

Christopher sat in his car outside the man's house. He had not eaten that morning and his insides were squirming with worry. This was the first time he had kept something important from his mother.

The house was small and there were scorch marks on the wall outside, where a barbecue or something must have gone on fire. The garden was more of a small weedy yard.

A woman answered the door and let him in once he explained who he was.

She was about ten years older than Christopher and a few inches taller. Her hair was in a ponytail and she wore a denim dress. She looked exhausted.

The woman asked him to take a seat. A grey mongrel was lying on his back on the front room rug as a young boy scratched it on the belly.

The woman brought in tea and some wrapped chocolate biscuits.

Christopher explained again who he was and launched into a long apologetic speech about the tragedy and how everyone was devastated about what had happened to the woman's husband. He spoke about how it was all the company's fault, even though his lawyers had told him not to, and he said they would do whatever it took and give her whatever she needed in an effort to make recompense for the terrible injuries that had befallen her husband. Christopher leaned forward during his unplanned speech, all the time looking at the boy and the dog. He rambled on about how he had lost interest in his work and in his life and how this terrible accident was really his fault and that his ignorance of the risks was no excuse and that he would never forgive himself and that he should never be forgiven by the woman or her family either.

By the end of it, his cheeks were wet and the woman's cheeks were wet and the young boy had to come to comfort his mother, and now his cheeks were wet too. Christopher would have loved to have hugged the boy and the boy's dog and the boy's mother and to have said or done something to unshatter their lives.

As he drove home afterwards, he could not recall clearly what he had said or what undertakings he had given. He only wished to drive fast, so fast that his life could not catch up with him.

Christopher stopped at the side of the road and vomited his misery into some nettles.

He could not face going back to his apartment and he was too ashamed to see his mother. Ashamed to tell her that because of him, a man with a young family had been left unrecognizable.

It was dark and moonless when he arrived at Ghost Mountain.

Ursula was alone in the house and her face was pale from crying when she opened the door. She pulled him close and sank deeply into him.

Christopher spent the night awake on the kitchen chair, listening to Ursula sleeping deeply in the next room.

Better in the Morning

The next morning, they ate a breakfast of brioche and coffee and Christopher walked around after his shower with his pigeon chest uncovered, looking for his tee shirt. Ursula thought his body looked doughy, not hard and hairy like a man's.

Ursula told him about her mother. She spoke casually as though she were talking to herself. It was not an unburdening. She hadn't planned to bring it up. She said she knew her mother would die but she didn't know how to prepare for her absence.

Christopher listened and ate his brioche. He said his shoulders were getting cold. Ursula realised she had been sitting on his tee shirt and handed it back to him. Ursula was sorry to see him cover up his pudgy belly. She would have liked to have kneaded it for the simple tactile pleasure of doing so.

Ursula washed a bunch of grapes and held them out to Christopher. He plucked them, grape by grape, and left the wet stalk in her palm.

They had been immersed in a consequenceless morning but now that it was time for him to leave, she began thinking about what would happen next. That even if Christopher ate grapes from the palm of her hand, it didn't mean she had control of him or herself.

"You need to go now. I have to paint," she said quietly.

"Are you going to paint Ghost Mountain?" he asked.

"I won't know what I'm painting until I start, but no, I'm not painting Ghost Mountain."

"Are you going to sell the wrestling picture?" he asked.

It had been the painting that had lost Ursula her boyfriend. He had thought she was making fun of him. That she was humiliating him.

"If you are going to sell it, I would give you whatever you want for it," said Christopher.

Ursula hesitated. She had never sold or given away a painting before. She was unprepared for the loss of it.

"You can borrow it," she said. "Don't hang it too high."

Christopher took it down gently and held it at arm's length.

Christopher had said very little the whole time he was there. Ursula did not know much about him these days, except what everyone knew. About his business and his money and his mother.

"What's your life like now, Christopher?" she asked.

Without lifting his eyes from the painting, he said, "There was an accident on a job and one of my men was injured in a blast. He will be unrecognisable if he lives. He has a wife and son."

"Is it your fault?" asked Ursula.

"Yes," said Christopher.

"What's going to happen?"

"His life will be ruined, his wife's life will be ruined and his son's life will be ruined."

"I meant, what's going to happen to you?" she asked.

Christopher continued to admire the picture. "You really got the position of the hips and the shoulders just right."

After Christopher had left, there was an absence in the house. He was gone and the wrestling painting was gone.

Ursula painted the absence.

She painted a portrait. A portrait of the unrecognisable man whose life had been ruined.

Pistol

Elaine had carried unresolved grief ever since she lost her first dog, Thelonious, who had choked on Ghost Mountain. That loss was a hard loss. Dominic was the only one who understood that, without which they might never have married and had Ursula. After Crabs died, Elaine swore that she could not bury another dog. The pain was too real and misunderstood. But now, she reasoned, any dog she brought home would outlive her. Elaine could hold two very different thoughts at once, or perhaps they were two aspects of the same thought. She could regret her own death but could appreciate that this provided the unexpected blessing of a new dog. This was no small joy.

Elaine wanted to get the dog so that Dominic would have company after she was gone. It would also be company for her when she got sicker and could no longer move. She would pass it slices of ham and when the pain came, she would distract herself by letting the dog lick salt from her hand. The dog would also be a friend to Ursula. It would be something that Dominic and Ursula could share. It would be a common responsibility and would stop them drifting apart.

Elaine asked her neighbour whether he had any dogs on his farm that might be suitable, or whether he knew of any dogs. The neighbour asked her the purpose of the dog. Elaine said she was dying and that it was to be a friend for her husband and daughter. The farmer was a practical man and did not enquire after her welfare. If she didn't need a guard dog or a hunting dog or a sheep dog or a rat-catching dog, then he thought he knew of one that might be suitable. This dog was a good-natured mongrel called Pistol. The woman who owned him was going into a residential home. Pistol was used to women, the farmer said.

Elaine reminded him that Pistol was for her husband.

The farmer said that Pistol wouldn't know the difference anyway, so who cares.

Elaine brought Pistol home and fed him the same dog food that Crabs used to eat. It gave Pistol the runs.

When Dominic came home he found Elaine cleaning up after Pistol.

"Who is this?" he asked.

Elaine introduced him to Pistol.

"I don't want a death dog," said Dominic.

"Don't call him that," said Elaine.

They brought Pistol for walks around Ghost Mountain, just like they had done with Crabs. They would meet Ursula there and do circuits of the base. Elaine no longer had the strength to climb it. Pistol would run up Ghost Mountain and chase around aimlessly, then bound back and report to Elaine when she called him.

Ursula said that Pistol was a little bit crazy but didn't seem dangerous.

Dominic said that Pistol had a sensitive digestive system.

Elaine was eating less and less, and retaining little of what she did eat. She had sympathy for Pistol.

On one of their late evening walks, Elaine started to tire and said she would sit for a while with the dog. That Dominic and Ursula shouldn't wait for her. She threw up in the nettles.

Ursula suggested they go back to the Ghost Mountain house, but Elaine said it was too far for her.

So Ursula said she would go and fetch some water and a blanket for Elaine.

Dominic wanted to wait with Elaine, but she said for him to go. She said that Ursula would worry less if she had Dominic with her.

After they had left, Elaine sat on a rock and rested her hands on her knees.

Then Elaine decided to kneel down and double over. The pain was marginally more bearable in that position.

When that became too much, she lay down.

Even though it was muddy, and she could feel a rock digging into her tailbone, she lay there and waited for what was happening.

When Ursula and Dominic returned, Elaine was already dead. Pistol was standing over her, licking the salty tears from her lifeless eyes.

Dipping Brioche

A cloud of midges hung in the air. Pistol lay at Dominic's feet. Elaine's death had happened. In a way, it was still happening.

Dominic rested on the rock that Elaine had been leaning on when they left her. Ursula knelt on her coat and held her dead mother's hand. She put the blanket over Elaine's face because of the midges.

There they stayed together, pooling their seriousness.

"I knew she would die, but still..." said Ursula.

They decided to spend the night with Elaine on Ghost Mountain. They would call the authorities in the morning.

After they had sat quietly for a time, they got chatting and Ursula explained to Dominic what had happened with her ex-boyfriend and the wrestling picture. She said that she and Christopher were close again.

She asked if she could text Christopher to tell him about Elaine.

Dominic said, of course.

Ghost Mountain was alive with early evening nature sounds. A bird hidden in the gorse was emitting a one note chirp like a failing smoke alarm. There was doppler buzzing from an unseen nearby insect. The wind susurrated through the grass, parting it one way, then the other.

Dominic teased a stick in front of Pistol and then threw it. Pistol didn't react.

Just as it was getting dark, Christopher approached Ghost Mountain with Martha, their raincoats making friction noises.

They had brought sleeping bags, blankets, a flask of coffee and some brioche.

"I'm sorry about your wife," said Martha. She shook hands with Dominic and passed him some coffee. It was the first coffee Dominic had drunk since he had switched to herbal tea in solidarity with Elaine.

Martha dipped her brioche in her coffee and the others all copied her and dipped theirs.

They sat and contemplated Elaine's covered body as though it were a campfire.

Christopher was sitting next to Ursula but not in an intimate way.

Every now and then someone would make an observation and it would be passed around for the others to add to it.

Pistol stood up, shook himself and wandered off.

Dominic asked Martha how she had been.

She answered in a natural, open way. Her corkscrew curls flickered in the wind as she spoke.

Ursula chatted quietly with Christopher, splitting the company into two conversations.

The quiet returned and each revisited what was inside them.

Dominic remembered that Pistol had been gone a long time. He stood up and shouted his name, cupping his hands around his mouth. Pistol bounded back to where they were and gambolled aimlessly, not directing his attention at anyone in particular.

Dominic called him over and scratched behind his ear.

"I think your dog might be blind," said Martha.

They talked in different formations throughout the night.

Dominic told Martha that what he feared most was the uneventfulness of his future.

Martha told Ursula that when her marriage ended it took her five years to recover. That Dominic would be dealing with the end of his marriage as well as the death of his wife.

Ursula told Dominic that she still had his front teeth in a matchbox by her bed.

Dominic told Martha that he would have liked more time but that he accepted there was never enough time with a person.

Ursula told Martha about the wrestling picture she had painted.

Dominic told Pistol he was a good boy even if he was blind.

Ursula told Pistol about Crabs.

Christopher was on the edge of everything and didn't talk much.

During the night, as the others slept, Dominic pulled back the blanket from Elaine's face and kissed her temples. She was cold and her skin was waxy. Her body was her body but it wasn't Elaine. Once he understood this, it made no sense to fight the tiredness. He replaced the blanket over her and stretched out on the grass. A rock underneath him protruded into his tailbone.

Wherever Elaine had gone to, she was not in the deep dreams that Dominic had that night.

Diesel

Dominic sat at home, reflecting on his own relevance. His house was now filled with Elaine's absence.

Pistol was there too and was pacing around. He sometimes bumped his hips off furniture but was not otherwise clumsy for a blind dog.

Dominic was no longer Elaine's husband. He was what was called a widower. That word felt new and also very old. It felt like a word that had been worn by many people and which was now offered to him to wear, even though it did not fit him. It felt too big and baggy and heavy. It was not tailored and had no lines. It was generic and it generically erased his past except for one event. My wife has died, it says. And that is who I am now. But that was not who Dominic was. What would Elaine have said if he went around thinking of himself that way? Elaine did not like family bullshit and she would not have liked widower bullshit. She would never have said to him, "Be a widower for me. Be my widower."

Dominic no longer felt like Ursula's father. She was an adult now. Dominic was no longer responsible for her needs. The relationship they had was now one of choice. Either could decide to end it. Just like Elaine had done with her estranged family and Dominic had done with his estranged family. Or maybe it had been the families who had estranged Elaine and Dominic. Dominic was not worried about estrangement from Ursula because they loved each other. After all, Ursula still had his front teeth in a matchbox. But their relationship was no longer a parental one. It was no longer irreversible. It was now in the realm of important but reversible things.

Over time, Dominic had ceased to be the town drunk, a husband and a father. Dominic considered the many people he had been but no longer was.

Dominic considered his body. The body that he had been inside for over seventy years. His hair was thinner and his muscle mass was decreasing. His front teeth were no longer his. For some twenty years they had been Ursula's. But if his body was not sovereign, if it could belong to other people, or if it could fade, and fade into something else that was not him, then he was not his body.

Perhaps all of these thoughts had occurred to him separately at different times in his life. But the thoughts had no power in that scattered formation. Now, assembled and ordered, they did have power. Just as letters have no meaning on their own but can be arranged in formation to acquire meaning as a word, so it was with these disparate thoughts.

Dominic considered Pistol. Pistol was blind. Had he always been blind or had he gone blind? His eyes were his own but without eyesight, it was as good as true that his eyes were not his own. Pistol didn't blink much. Dominic supposed that it was because of his blindness. This meant that midges bothered him more. Pistol would walk into midge clouds. The midges would fly into his eyes causing him irritation.

Pistol was giddy and perhaps needed to wee. Dominic usually waited until night before bringing Pistol for his walk. At dusk there were midge clouds everywhere, which wouldn't suit Pistol, but because he was blind, he didn't mind walking in the dark.

Dominic brought Pistol outside, without a leash. Pistol peed a hot gush in the driveway.

They headed down the country road together, Pistol walking along the centre line. Dominic wondered how he knew where the centre was. Perhaps by the camber.

Dominic let Pistol lead.

Dominic wanted to know what it felt like to be a blind dog. Walking in the dark was not the same as being blind. The dark was uneven and there were degrees of blackness that provided silhouettes and shadows, which brought definition to what he could see. Dominic closed his eyes and walked behind Pistol. Yes, he could feel the camber of the road!

A diesel engine thrummed in the distance. It was satisfying to recognise it. The noise was moving behind the roadside hedges. The roads around there had been laid across a boggy landscape. They rose and sank unevenly, bouncing drivers in their seats. They were narrow too. Cars drove closer to the centre of the road unless passing. The jeopardy was exciting. Dominic could hear Pistol's breathing. Pistol's eyes would be open but sightless. His own eyes remained shut.

Here I am – a widower in the middle of the road! he thought.

The car was directly ahead. Its headlights filtered pink and yellowy light through Dominic's eyelids. It shone brighter as the distance shortened. The engine noise became louder, clearer, nearer.

Am I a widower now? Am I a husband? Am I a father? What is the difference between Pistol and me, really? If we are both hit by a car, will any of our differences matter?

These thoughts were cycling through Dominic's brain as the car passed him so closely that the gust unbalanced him. The diesel sound had intensified to a roar and now it faded behind him.

He opened his eyes and was relieved to see Pistol still padding ahead of him.

He thought about what Elaine would have said about risking himself like this. About risking Pistol too. She would have accused him of drama. His exhilaration faded into a minor shame.

At home that night, Pistol slept on the landing.

In bed, Dominic could not sleep. He tried to discover himself, but it felt wrong to think of Elaine in that way now. He thought about Martha instead but those thoughts could not progress because he kept wondering whether Elaine was somewhere where she could see his thoughts. Where she could see his crushes. The crushes she had surely known about.

This was how Dominic's first day of coping with Elaine's absence had gone.

Ashes

Elaine had left instructions that after she died, Dominic and Ursula were to throw her ashes over their shoulders. She said this was because she did not want them to use her death as an excuse to look backwards in their lives. Elaine also said that she did not want her ashes spread in a special place. The site of their dispersal should not assume symbolic status. It was not to become a place that they visited in remembrance of her.

Elaine had thought people did too much remembering. She was a highly logical person, but her views were also informed by mistakes she had made when spending too much of her life missing those she had lost, including her dogs, Thelonious and Crabs. She understood the dangers of over-remembering.

In her own way, Elaine had tried to be happy and to make other people happy, though she would have been the first to admit that such things did not come to her naturally. She did not want all her effort undermined by her becoming a source of sadness after she died.

Losing his wife had made Dominic a little strange and eccentric even. He had once gone walking on Ghost Mountain wearing only his dressing gown and slippers.

Ursula hoped that this was just a phase.

Ursula had been feeling the displacement that comes with grief. It was not like sadness or upset. It was more like homesickness. Like she wasn't where she should be and couldn't get there. She felt dreamy and unfocused. She found it hard to finish what she started, whether books, cooking, tidying up or painting. Especially painting.

Ursula had wanted to recreate the scene on Ghost Mountain the night Elaine had died. She wanted to paint it as a nativity scene. The first figure she painted was Pistol but it was hard to convey his blindness in the painting.

The picture lay on her kitchen table, unfinished. In truth, it was practically unstarted.

As they walked with Pistol on Ghost Mountain, Ursula asked Dominic where they should spread Elaine's ashes.

Dominic suggested spreading them on Ghost Mountain, near the rock where she had died.

Ursula thought that was too symbolic. She suggested the garden of their house.

Dominic said it was too overgrown. They had neglected it. He and Elaine liked the idea of a garden but not the reality of gardening. Their garden was full of incorrigible weeds. Elaine would not want to be scattered among the weeds she had so often cursed.

Ursula stopped for a moment and said she felt dizzy. She threw up in the nettles.

Dominic asked if she was OK.

Dominic asked if it was morning sickness and if she was pregnant.

"How did you know?" asked Ursula.

"Elaine was really sick when she was pregnant with you," he said. "And you are sleeping with Christopher, so these things happen."

Ursula said she had not slept with Christopher. They were close, but not in that way. She asked Dominic whether she could ask Christopher to say that he was the father? She would not ask Christopher for anything more than that. She didn't want her ex-boyfriend involved.

Ursula felt like crying. She hadn't planned to tell anyone but now it all came out because she couldn't keep it in anymore. Just like the vomit which was now steaming on the nettles.

Dominic held her close. Ursula apologised that her breath was smelly after getting sick, but Dominic said it was no worse than Pistol's breath. Dominic called Pistol over and they hugged him too as he panted.

"I was already pregnant when Elaine died," said Ursula. "Though I didn't know then. It was a shame. I could have told her."

"Don't look backwards," said Dominic.

Mother Gap

Ursula was painting Elaine's death scene.

She had painted Pistol and she had painted Dominic, though had not yet started on the details of his face. She had not made up her mind whether to depict the gap in his teeth. To depict him as Elaine had done. To make her painting speak to Elaine's painting. Elaine's ashes were in a plain urn on the table beside her. The ashes exerted no direct influence and yet made a difference. Was the difference creative rain? Ursula was unsure. There was nobody to ask about creative rain. Was it a feeling? Was it a sensation? Elaine would have known.

Christopher came in through the back door and sat down heavily in the kitchen chair.

He did not announce himself and Ursula did not interrupt her painting.

Ursula refused to disturb herself.

She paused a moment and wiped her brush with a rag. She searched around her.

Christopher rose from his seat and picked up the jar of safflower oil that was by the leg of her chair. He held it up to her.

Ursula dipped her brush in the oil and began cleaning the paint from it. Christopher stood beside her as she did so.

When she returned to painting, Christopher sat down again, still holding the jar for her for when she needed it next. He knew not to look at the painting. He knew not to look at Ursula while she was painting.

Eventually, Ursula put down her brush and stared at the picture for a long time. She was not analysing it or thinking about it particularly. She was looking at it the way a person looks at a fire. With distance and elsewhereness.

Christopher spoke from behind her and told her that the man with the unrecognisable face had died.

Ursula told him that she was pregnant.

A silence resumed between them.

The tension between them was like the tension on the string of an instrument. The tension was essential to whatever happened next.

Ursula could feel that the picture she was painting was not a true picture. It was merely bait to draw out what was really inside her. She never knew what her intentions were. She had to give her intentions form before she could see what they were. That's all her paintings were. The waste product of her intentions.

To the gap in her life that she had always felt, was added the gap of Elaine's death. Now Ursula would step forward into the gap. The mother gap. Her baby would fill the space she vacated.

She cooked stir fry for her and Christopher. She had enough chicken for one but stretched it by adding butter beans. Chicken and butter bean stir fry. Her fingers still had paint on them as she cut the chicken. Even when she washed her hands after handling the meat, the paint still stained her fingertips.

Becoming a mother didn't faze Ursula.

She had been brought up without family bullshit.

A person could not be expected to become someone else simply because they were now in a family.

The child would call her Ursula.

She wouldn't lie to the child.

If she punished her child, she wouldn't make anger part of the punishment.

Ursula would not try to be wise or exemplary.

They would eat chicken and when they didn't have enough chicken they would add butter beans.

There was only one question she couldn't answer alone.

She asked Christopher to agree to say that he was the father. That if anyone asked, he would look them in the eye and say the child was his.

Christopher too had a gap. Where his father was meant to be. Now Christopher would step forward into that gap. The father gap.

And Ursula's baby would fill the space he vacated.

The Butcher's Flat

Christopher had located his father.

He had not been hard to find, though the motivation to look for him had been hard to find.

All this time, Christopher's father had not been far away. He had been within touching distance but had not made contact. He had been within earshot of Christopher's success but remained unprompted.

Christopher reflected on what this lack of interest said to him.

Did it boil his childhood?

Christopher waited in the queue at the butchers.

He listened to the butcher making small talk. Meat-related small talk and other small talk, after which, the butcher would hand the customer a ticket with blood on it and they would pay at the front of the shop.

When it came to his turn, Christopher said he did not want meat. He was looking to speak to the man who lived in the flat upstairs. He explained who he was, and in doing so, explained who his father was too.

The butcher said that he owned the flat upstairs. The man was his tenant.

There was a queue behind Christopher but the butcher didn't hurry him.

Christopher asked whether his father was a train driver. The last time he had seen him it was a long time ago. Christopher was just a child. His father had been wearing a uniform from the crosstown train company.

The butcher said his father worked for them, but it was a job related to mapping. He was a surveyor or something like that. He had been the Clerk of Maps once. He still had a theodolite. He asked whether Christopher knew what that was?

Christopher said he did.

The butcher said that he was his father's son, alright, if he knew what a theodolite was. Not many people did. The butcher said that Christopher did not look like him though.

Christopher explained that his corkscrew curls were from his mother's side.

The butcher said he did indeed remember his mother.

Christopher waited outside the butcher's in his car and watched the door to the upstairs flat. The flat's doorbell had a blank nameplate.

It was early evening when his father arrived home.

He looked the same. Lean and sallow with heavy shadow.

Christopher approached him and said who he was.

His father had been drinking.

They were the same height.

His father said he recognised Christopher and invited him inside.

The stairs were uneven. The landing light didn't work and his father had to experiment to find the right key.

He made Christopher a chicken sandwich. He made one for himself too. As he lay it before Christopher on a worn table with scattered tobacco flakes on it, he said there was only one chicken breast but it was enough for two. He said he bought it from the butcher downstairs.

Christopher's father opened a can of generic supermarket lager. Christopher said he was driving and took a mug of tea instead. His father said the milk was off and served the tea to him black.

The flat was tired looking. There were maps on the walls, unframed and held up with thumb tacks. A theodolite lay on the couch beside Christopher. Its tripod was still standing across the room, like a third person in their company.

His father ate his sandwich. His jacket was still on. Christopher had taken his off and noticed that the flat was cold.

Christopher said he was going to become a father.

"I had no idea you were even married," said his father.

"I am not married," said Christopher.

His father dusted the crumbs from his fingers onto the carpet.

"The mother is named Ursula," volunteered Christopher. "Her father used to work with you when you were the Clerk of Maps."

His father looked like he was thinking. Not reacting. Just thinking.

Christopher hadn't touched his sandwich.

"So, it's the town drunk's girl?" his father asked.

"Don't call her that," said Christopher, seriously, "and don't call him that."

His father apologised.

"I am estranging you," said Christopher. He wasn't sure if that was the correct way of saying it. "You are not my father anymore. I will be the father now. That's all I wanted to say."

His father considered this peculiar speech.

"You are lucky to be able to have kids," his father said eventually. "I was not that fortunate."

Christopher had drunk some tea. He held it in his mouth without swallowing.

"I can't have children. I was never able to have children," his father said.

Christopher's father picked a hair from his trousers and then sat back.

"So, your wish is granted," his father said. "I am not your father. You can estrange me all you like. You don't owe me any explanation or visit. And more importantly, I don't owe you anything."

Christopher felt as though he had turned into papier-mâché. Like he would crumple if he was touched.

"In case nobody has had the guts to tell you," his former father continued, "the town drunk is your father. I'm sorry, Dominic is your father. He and your mother had a thing. A brief thing, but long enough. After all, these things don't necessarily take long."

"You're lying," said Christopher, his voice cracking. "He would have said something."

"Does he know?"

Christopher's former father smiled a wolf smile. With his mouth but not his eyes. "That girl is your sister, or half-sister," he said in a playful voice.

Christopher's father lifted Christopher's chicken sandwich and began to eat it.

"What a strange little boy you are," his former father said, spitting chicken as he spoke.

Christopher felt like a balloon. As though he had no insides.

"Sleeping with your sister ..."

Christopher's childhood was boiling. He looked inside himself. Christopher, Christopher, where are you?

"... and sleeping with your mother."

Boiling, boiling childhood. Where are you, Christopher? Christopher! Christopher!

The chicken flew from his former father's mouth as the theodolite broke his jaw. The sound was somewhere between a crack and a snap.

Ghost Mountain

It was dusk at Ghost Mountain. The leverets scattered beneath the buzzard hanging in the air.

Ursula was working on the painting of Elaine's death scene when the sharp pains started. There was spotting on her underwear.

Christopher's former father's jaw hung loose, like a gate. He held Christopher tightly in a headlock. Christopher's windpipe was clamped. He couldn't breathe.

The buzzard hovered as if suspended by a string. In the grass beneath, there were two leverets crouched low with their ears pressed back.

Ursula rang Christopher but his phone was not answering. She called Dominic. She was on her hunkers. The pain was a stabbing pain. Dominic said he was at the vet. Pistol was indeed blind but otherwise healthy.

The pressure around Christopher's neck was affecting the blood flow to his brain. He turned in towards his former father to work a gap so he could breathe. He tried separating his former father's interlocking grip. He even attempted to lift him. Christopher's head was truly locked. The moves he had learned from watching wrestling on his computer had not worked.

The grass on Ghost Mountain was long but too sparse to conceal the leverets.

Dominic brought Ursula to the hospital. He explained the situation to the man at reception. The man said he was only a security guard and called a nurse. There was confusion as Dominic confirmed that yes, he was the father. He meant he was Ursula's father. The nurse meant the baby's father. Ursula was in agony.

Christopher's former father would not relent. He was angry. Viciously angry. Christopher became calm. The situation was inescapable. It was up to his former father how long it went on.

The two leverets did not disperse. The buzzard could only hunt one of them.

Ursula lay on the examination table. She had a pillow between her legs. There was spotting on the pillow. Dominic had left Pistol in the car. He didn't know whether to stay or go.

Christopher realised that he would never escape the headlock. That the rest of his life would be spent in that headlock. The very short time he had left in his life would pass that way.

The buzzard played in the eddies and returned to its hovering point. The two leverets were hypnotised by its movements.

Ursula lay back. She let out a scream that came from deep inside her. It came from her whole body, like it had been building since she was born and contained everything in her life. It was her life scream.

Christopher had always wondered how and when he would die. And now he knew. His death would be the end of all his curiosity.

The buzzard was still. Its tail was fanned in readiness. The leverets too were still.

Ursula wondered whether this feral pain meant that she would die and that her child would die. Again her body screamed its life scream.

Christopher's childhood seemed so far away. His whole sense of himself seemed distant. In the choking calm, his name echoed around the emptiness inside him – Christopher! Christopher!

The buzzard lifted in an updraught, ready to strike below.

Ursula's body again screamed its life scream. Words were whispering deep inside her body. The words crawled onto her dry, cracked lips. The words were a mantra. Ursula whispered the mantra. I know I will live and I know my child will live. I know I will live and I know my child will live. I know I will live and I know my child will live.

In the headlock, Christopher was dizzy and breathless. As he drifted, he could hear his name resounding in the cavernous emptiness – Christopher! Christopher!

And Ghost Mountain was Ghost Mountain.

Acknowledgements

Thank you to my wife, Sinéad, for all your loving support and patience as I worked on this book.

My love to my two sons, Jacob and Thomas, for making me laugh and telling me interesting things every day.

My sincere thanks to Kevin and Hetha Duffy and everyone at Bluemoose Books for your hard work, good humour and encouragement, and for trusting me to express my exploded heart.

My gratitude, as always, to my editor, Lin Webb, for your perspicacious and sensitive input, and for the way you have taught me – over the course of three books (so far) – to see my own writing more clearly.

Every writer needs good friends, with whom to tease out doubts. My sincere thanks to Michael Stevens and Jackie Lynam for your feedback, friendship and for hearing me out.

I owe a huge debt to my dear friend, David Collard. Your online artistic gatherings of *A Leap in the Dark*, *Carthorse Orchestra* and *The Glue Factory* saved my creative life during the pandemic and exposed me to a rich community of talented writers. It was my "Moveable Feast."

My heartfelt thanks to Tom Climent for permitting us to use your luminous painting, which captures in one image what I tried to say in 280 pages.

Thanks once again to Fiachra McCarthy for the sensitive and striking cover design.

Thank you to everyone who has read, written about and championed my work.

Please support your local bookshops and libraries.